**She couldn't believe it. They were supposed to have a future together. He wasn't supposed to die…**

It was August, two months before Evan was supposed to be coming home. Clare was sitting at her office desk when she heard a knock on her door. "Come on in," she said. It was a very informal work situation.

She was surprised to see her mother and father walk through the door. She sat there a moment staring at them. "What's wrong, Daddy?" she asked.

They continued looking at her, as if the burden of the news they carried was too much to convey.

Clare started crying, sobbing. "Tell me what's happened, something's happened, what is it?"

They came over to her and she stood up and went into their arms.

"Honey," her mother said, "we just talked to Evan's parents. They received word from Evan's company that negotiations had broken down with the rebels. They were being aggressively pursued by the Indonesian Army. They think the men might have attempted to escape, they don't know for sure, but the men were killed, Clare. I'm so sorry, darling."

Clare is a twenty-four-year-old woman who faces life with quiet confidence and inner turmoil. She experiences love, hurt and uncertainty, sexual harassment in the workplace, and tragedy. She meets and falls in love with Evan Garner in their first year of college. But after graduation, Evan contracts to work for an oil company for two years in Indonesia while Clare goes to work for the City of Denver, Colorado, and waits for his return. When the love of her life is reported killed, she is devastated and struggles to find reason to go on. Finally, believing she will never be happy again, she agrees to settle for a life with a man she knows she will never love. But her life takes a dramatic turn, at its darkest point, just before the dawn...

# KUDOS for *Clare*

TAYLOR JONES SAYS: In *Clare* by Jack Sprouse, Clare is a twenty-four-year-old beauty whose boyfriend has gone overseas for two years to earn his fortune, leaving Clare at home to wonder if he is ever coming home. When he disappears and is presumed dead, Clare is convinced that she will never know happiness again. Making some bad choices, Clare seems determined to make this a self-fulfilling prophecy. The story is cute clever, and charming, filled with delightful characters with plenty of surprises to keep you on your toes. ~ *Taylor Jones, The Review Team of Taylor Jones & Regan Murphy*

REGAN MURPHY SAYS: Clare by Jack Sprouse is the story of young woman from a warm and loving home and a young man from a cold and aloof one. When these two fall in love, there are bound to be problems, and there are. Clare, our heroine, needs to hear Ethan, our hero, say that he loves her, but that is something that Ethan seems unable to do. Still, it is assumed by both of them that they will marry. Then, when Ethan graduates from college, he takes a job with an oil company overseas hoping that he can make enough money to buy the two of them a home in the mountains. But things go badly for Ethan and Clare is left not knowing if he is alive or dead. Now she doesn't think she can go on without him.

Clare is a charming and intriguing story, told in a refreshing voice. The characters are well developed and realistic, and the plot has some clever surprises. ~ *Regan Murphy, The Review Team of Taylor Jones & Regan Murphy*

# CLARE

A Novel

Jack Sprouse

*A Black Opal Books Publication*

GENRE: WOMEN'S FICTION/ROMANCE/FAMILY LIFE

First Publication: JUNE 2017

Published by Black Opal Books **http://www.blackopalbooks.com**

*This book is dedicated to my granddaughters*
*Cheyenne Middleton*
*Cami Middleton*
*Marcy Hefner*

# PROLOGUE

## *Will*

Will Cain arrived at Brunswick Naval Air Station in August of 1960. He was alone and belonged only to the navy. He had no aspirations at the time of being anything but a naval aviator, traveling the world, and being free. During his tour of duty, he deployed to Guantanamo Bay to expel the Russians from Cuba at the behest of President John Kennedy. He spent five months in Sigonella, Sicily, and made numerous deployments to various parts of the world.

He came to believe that there was no greater calling on earth than that of a combat aircrew member on a navy patrol aircraft.

He remained of such a mind until he met Jamie Dunham, a local girl who lived with her family in Brunswick. Then his world changed forever.

Will mustered out of the navy in February of 1964. He left Brunswick, pulling a small U-Haul trailer, carrying what few belongings he had, along with Jamie, and their five-month old daughter whom they named Clare, after the café where the two of them had met, and he went home to Colorado.

The family lived in a rented house in Lakewood for several years, eventually saving the money to buy a house in the same neighborhood, while adding a son in 1966, Will worked for his father, learning how to manage one of his five hardware stores, and eventually took over management of the entire chain of stores in 1973 when his father took a reduced role in the business.

Will built a new home in an area of Coal Creek Canyon, above Golden, Colorado, where he had often hiked and camped with his dog Boxer when he was a kid. A life-long dream was fulfilled when he moved his family into the house in Coal Creek Canyon.

# CHAPTER 1

*Clare*

Clare Cain was sitting at a table in the Student Center Building of Colorado University, pretending to be studying her classwork. Her bright blue eyes were alternately glancing from the page of her biology textbook to the front door of the building, hoping to see Evan Garner walk through the door. She continued her attempts to read the lesson while her peripheral vision informed her every time someone entered the building, drawing her attention away again. It was frustrating, Evan was frustrating.

He was like a child sometimes, she thought, easily

distracted. He might have passed some friends who were playing flag football and had gotten into the game with them, for all she knew. While she sat there, steaming, Evan was off somewhere else, doing no telling what.

They had fallen in love in their first year at CU, at least she had fallen in love with Evan and had assumed he had fallen for her as well. He certainly acted like he was in love with her. He was a caring boy, very considerate, opened doors for her, and kissed her hands frequently. He looked at her lovingly. She came to believe that he was just too shy to tell her he loved her. Evan was one of the few boys she'd dated who hadn't gone insane over her mother. After commenting one time, the first time she took him home to meet her parents, that he could see why Clare was so beautiful, he'd never made another remark about Jamie Cain.

Clare looked like her mother, blonde hair and blue eyes and of slender build, but she was not as pretty. It was a source of annoyance and pride at the same time that her mother, at forty years old, was still just as beautiful as she was when she married Clare's father Will.

Theirs had been a storybook marriage, and Clare wanted the same for her and Evan. But lately, she had begun to wonder if it would ever happen for them. They talked as if they were making plans for the future, but Evan never actually spoke the words Clare needed to hear.

They made love two months after they started dating.

It was a wonderful thing for her, and she knew it was for him too. He told her that, very profusely and many times. Since then they had been sleeping together on a regular basis. Sometimes she almost wished she would get pregnant so they would have to get married. But her cooler head prevailed, and she started taking birth control pills so she could finish college before thinking about anything past that.

Finally, her attention was drawn to the front door again and, this time, she saw the slow ambling gait of her love interest coming into the building. He looked around to see her waving to him, and he started walking toward her table.

"Hello, beautiful," he said, took her hand, and kissed it.

"My, my," she said, in a mock Southern accent, placing the back of her hand to her forehead. "I do believe I might swoon."

"Save it for later, I'm taking you up to Nederland for dinner."

"Nederland? I can't go to Nederland tonight," she said. "I have tests tomorrow. I have to study."

"Sorry, my friend Cal is managing Neapolitans tonight, and he's holding a table for us if we can get there at seven. We won't have to wait, like we usually do.

"But I have to study," she said, perplexed.

"No, you don't. You know it can take hours to get a table in Neos, but tonight we can walk right in. We can't pass up this opportunity. Besides, you love the drive up the canyon."

Neapolitans Italian Restaurant in Nederland, Colorado, was a very popular eating establishment in the early eighties, despite its remote location. It was about sixteen miles from the campus to Nederland but took approximately twenty-five minutes because of the mountain road, depending on if you were going up or coming down. It was well worth the trip because the food at Neapolitans was really good. The wait, however, could be excruciating on a Saturday night.

"Oh, and by the way, my folks are coming in this weekend," he told her. "They want to take us out to dinner. Can you be here?"

"I haven't been home in a while," Clare said. "Daddy wants me to spend the weekend with the family. Can you bring them by our house for a social visit? I'd like to meet them and my mom and dad would too, I know they would."

"Maybe so. I'll give you a call."

"Okay," she said. "I hope you do."

After dinner, they walked out past a long line of customers waiting to get into the restaurant. Clare smiled as she passed them, feeling like a princess, and displaying an air of privilege and exclusivity that came from having a reserved table at a restaurant that didn't take reservations.

They stopped at the Barker Reservoir and made out

for about half an hour until she pushed him away. "I do have to study, Evan," she said. "I'm serious."

"Okay," he said. He started the engine and headed back down Boulder Canyon. "I'll see you Saturday night at your house," he told her when he dropped her off at her apartment.

"Good," she said and got out of his car. "I love you," she added but he didn't hear her as he drove off.

Saturday evening, Clare was standing at the window of the Cain home, watching for Evan. Traffic was always light in the remote mountain neighborhood and, each time a car approached up the road, she became hopeful. She was actually surprised when a car pulled into their driveway. She had not expected him to show up. Evan was driving, his father was in the passenger seat, and his mother in the back seat. Evan was an only child, a fact which Clare was convinced had caused his inability to demonstrate feelings and sensitivity.

Mr. Garner was about the same height as his son, balding and with a slight paunch around his mid-section. He looked to be about fifty years-old, eight years older than her father, Will. Evan's mother was an attractive woman of about the same age with brownish blonde hair. She later learned that Evan's father was fifty-two and his mother was forty-nine at the time. Will and Jamie met them at the door and congenialities were exchanged all around. Jamie Cain took the older Garners into the den to where she had set up drinks and refreshments.

Evan and Jamie "James," Clare's brother, immediately went off to Jamie's room to check out Jamie's new rifle or fishing pole, or some other man thing, all to Clare's consternation. The two boys were kindred spirits and had gone on hunting trips together each summer into the mountains for a week at a time, since the first time they met.

After dinner, both families gathered on the patio to talk and catch up. It was generally accepted that their two children would one day be married so they would become an extended family.

"As I have said before, Will, you have a beautiful home here, " George said. "I'd love to live in the mountains, but my job won't allow it."

"Thank you, George. It can be some trouble in the winter getting up and down the canyon but we've learned to cope. I grew up in Lakewood and had always loved coming up here. I promised myself that I'd build a house in the mountains one day. The kids were raised here. They seem to like it okay."

"Evan loves the mountains too," George replied. I expect he'll follow your lead one day.

"Evan's a nice young man," Will replied. "He doesn't say much and I read that as a positive. Mostly I judge him on what my daughter tells me about him."

"He has some big ideas, bigger than his budget right now, but Evan's not afraid of hard work. I expect he'll do well. It's a struggle putting him through school but he works every summer and saves his money to help us out. He's pretty crazy about Clare, I know that for sure."

"He's all she talks about," Will said, laughing. "Sometimes I can't shut her up."

George chuckled about that and nodded his head.

"And he's become good friends with my son James—Jamie, I mean," Will continued. "We call him James so as not to confuse him with his mother. We named him after her but didn't realize at the time what confusion that would cause. We couldn't call him Junior and calling him Jamie just created havoc, so, we call him James."

"Makes sense to me," George said. "Anyway, Will, if Evan and Clare end up getting married, then his mother and I couldn't be more proud to have her for a daughter-in-law."

"Thank you, George, we feel the same way about Evan. If he makes Clare happy then we are happy too." They raised their tea glasses together and toasted that.

The Garners left around 10:00 for the drive back to Greeley. Evan kissed Clare goodbye and said he would see her for lunch on Monday. As always it seemed she was left with something wanting. Evan was caring and attentive but he never told her he loved her. She sensed that he did but he never said it. It had become an ache that just wouldn't go away.

She left on Sunday night, and returned to her apartment and went to bed early so she'd be rested for her early class in Human Culture, one of the electives required for her BA degree in Sociology. Although she had always been a daddy's girl, Clare was more politically aligned with her mother, who had been a school teacher for much of her married life. Clare's father, having been born and raised in Colorado, was more the conservative than was Jamie Cain, the girl he had fallen in love with while he was in the navy, stationed in the state of Maine. Nevertheless, politics was never a topic of conversation in the Cain household.

When Clare first told her father she wanted to major in Sociology, he simply asked her what that meant and what she would be doing to make money.

"Sociology is the scientific study of human social behavior, Daddy," she told him. "It's all about how society influences individuals and how individuals influence society."

"That sounds like it came right out of the college pamphlet." Will replied.

She smiled at him and nodded her head. "Yeah, it did."

"If that's what you want to do, baby, then I'm okay with it. Now what will you do once you get your degree?"

"I can work in government research or data analysis, either state or federal. Or I can work in the private sector as a counselor, or maybe I might want to be a writer. I think it pays pretty good money."

"Well, I'm sure your husband will appreciate that."

"If I ever get one," she said, pouting.

"Oh, come on, honey," Will said. "You're a beautiful, intelligent young woman. You'll meet the right man one day. Look at your dad. I met the perfect woman for me, and I was just a navy flyboy with no apparent future or redeemable qualities, and yet it happened. It will happen for you too, I guarantee it."

"Thank you, Daddy, I love you."

"I love you too, baby. Don't worry. The problem is not finding a husband for you, the problem is finding one good enough for you. That, young lady, is a tall order."

"Mom found the perfect man, I just hope I can too," she said, smiling at him.

"Oh, now you're not playing fair. How much do you need?"

Clare started laughing. "I don't need any money, Daddy, but thanks, anyway."

A month or so after she had begun her first semester she was in the Student Center having a snack and a coke when she noticed a boy staring at her from a nearby table. She smiled at him. He smiled back, weakly, but made no other attempt to communicate with her. He was cute, she thought, not handsome but very cute. His brown hair was cut just over his ears and to the collar in back but neatly combed. He appeared to be a couple of inches shorter than her father, she decided, when he stood up and walked away from his table. She half expected him to come over to her table and talk to her but he didn't. He just left the building.

Three days later she went back to the Student Center, and there he was again, sitting at the same table staring at her.

She stared back at him and smiled again. This time he stood up and started walking toward her. He didn't sit down but stood across from her on the other side of the table and spoke to her.

"I guess I'm going to have to get your schedule, I've been in here every day this week waiting for you and finally, you show up. If I eat any more pie, I'm going to be as fat as a house."

She put her hand over her mouth and giggled. "I thought it was just fate that you happened to be here the very day I decided to come in to study, but now you tell me you planned this. I'm flattered, I suppose, unless you're a serial killer. You're not a serial killer, are you?"

"No," he said, "I just wanted to meet you."

"And why did you want to meet me?"

"For the most basic of reasons, I guess," he said. "You're incredibly pretty and I was hoping we could go out sometime."

"I'd like that, so yes, we can. My name is Clare, Clare Cain. Why don't you sit down?"

He pulled out the chair across from her and sat down in it. "I'm Evan Garner from Greeley and I'm glad to meet you, Clare. Are you from Colorado?"

"Yes," she replied. "I live with my family near Golden in Coal Creek Canyon. I have a one-room apartment on Colorado Avenue here in town. But I usually go home most weekends."

"I'm living in the dorm, at least for my first year. I can't afford to live off campus right now."

"What are you studying, Evan?" she asked him.

"I want to be a petroleum engineer."

"Wow, you must be very smart," she said.

"My mother tells me I am."

"Then it must be so," she responded. "Mothers don't lie."

"Then yours must have told you that you'd be able to beguile young men, because that's what you did to me before I ever came over to your table."

"Oh, now I'm going to have to use a term my daddy taught me," she said, giggling.

"Are the initials B and S?" he asked.

"Exactly," she said, still giggling.

"Okay, then give me another chance. Perhaps I came on a little too strongly. You got my attention at the other table. I wasn't beguiled until I sat down across from you at your table."

"All right, Mister Garner," she said. "I'll buy a pound of that."

He chuckled. "That sounds like another something your father might say."

"It is. He's got a million of them."

"Well I hope to meet him some day," Evan said.

"Oh, I'm sure that can be arranged," she said.

They dated regularly for two months and, even before they had gone to bed together, Evan treated her like she was made of gold, opening doors for her and showering her with attention. He brought her gifts and flowers, and seemed content to just be with her. His favorite place to eat was up in Boulder Canyon at an Italian Restaurant called Neapolitans in Nederland, Colorado. They usually went during the week because the place was very small and it was next to impossible to get a table on Saturday night.

He came to her apartment often to study with her or to watch television. They always made out, but it wasn't until one Friday night when it had become more intense than usual that she asked him if he wanted to stay the night.

"If you want me too, I do," he said.

"I want you to," she said. Taking his hand, she led him into her bedroom. She took off her clothes very quickly and got into the bed and under the covers just as quickly. He smiled at her as he took off his clothes and got in next to her.

"This is your first time?" he asked her.

She nodded. "Yes."

"Don't worry, Clare," he told her as he took her in his arms. "You're safe with me. You'll always be safe with me."

She marveled at the wonderful thing that was happening to her. Evan was incredible—gentle and tender. It was clear this was not his first time but she didn't care. She was in love, hopelessly. She knew it and knew that he had to know it, too. She walked around in a daze for the next few days.

Evan didn't seem all that changed by the close encounter, but he kept telling her incessantly how wonderful she was and that no one and nothing had ever made him feel like she did. He started calling her pet names—baby, honey, darling, pumpkin, but he never said, "I love you." She had to assume that it would come in due time.

Her mother figured it out right away that she and Evan were sleeping together but her father never did, or if he did, he chose to go right on pretending that his little girl was still as pure as the driven snow. That's how daddies are, she thought.

They graduated in 1986 and Evan applied for a job with American oil and Exploration Company. He was offered a position that would take him overseas for two years with no return trip until the contract was up, to take advantage of a no-taxes perk agreement that the government had offered the company.

Clare was devastated. She was hoping he would suggest they get married before he left but he did not. He asked her to wait for him. "Please Clare, please wait for me. I'll write you and I'll send tape recordings telling you all about what I'm doing, and you can do the same. It will only be two years and, when I get back, I'll have enough money to buy us a house free and clear. This is what I've always wanted to do. It's what I spent four years in school for. Please promise me you'll wait."

She told him she would wait for him but she almost hated him for accepting a job that would take him away from her for so long. She began sending her resume out to various companies in the Denver area, hoping she could live at home and commute back and forth and not have to live by herself in a lonely apartment.

She met Evan at Stapleton the day he flew out of her life for what would surely seem like an eternity. What would have been a special moment for her, was spoiled by Evan's parents being there. She had not thought that out, although she should have realized that he could not have driven his car to the airport and then just left it there. He didn't tell her he loved her but neither did he tell his folks he loved them, not even his mother.

This was a strange family, the Garners, Clare thought. They were so different from the one in which she grew up. She was constantly being told, "I love you, Clare, or Mommy loves you, Clare." Her daddy called her Clare bear, he spelled it b-a-r-e on occasion because she often ran around the house without her clothes a lot when she was the only child. "Daddy loves Clare bear," he was always telling her. Then when her brother came along, the "I love you" comments were multiplied times two. Neither of the Cain children ever had the slightest doubt that they were loved by their parents, and by each other. Clare grew up in a world of love, and it pained her to realize that the love of her life, Evan Garner, apparently had not.

She told his parents that she would stay in touch. They each promised to pass on any news they received from Evan to the other one. They watched together, as the plane left Denver and flew out of sight, and then she bid them goodbye.

# CHAPTER 2

*Lakewood*

*1964*:

Jamie Cain picked up her five-month old daughter, Clare, from out of the car seat and held her up to the window of the U-Haul truck lumbering down I-95. "Look, Clare," she said, smiling at her husband Will who was driving. "Say goodbye to Maine. We're going to our new home in Colorado."

"She's five-months old, honey, I don't think she'll remember this," Will said.

"I know. I just want to be able to tell her about it when she gets older."

"Are you sorry to be leaving?" he asked her.

"No, Will, I'm not, just a little sad I suppose."

"I am, too, Jamie. I love this place. I met you here and we had Clare here. This place changed my life, saved it in many ways. We'll come back often, I promise you."

"I know, and I'm looking forward to starting our life in Colorado. Clare and I have never been there, you know."

"Uh, yeah, I know that," he said, smiling first at her then at the baby.

It was a long grueling trip through Ohio, Indiana, Illinois, and Missouri, then over the Mississippi River. Jamie marveled at things she had never seen before. When they crossed into Kansas, Will said he could see the mountains.

"Oh, you cannot," Jamie said and Will laughed at her. He pointed at his head to indicate he could see them in his mind.

Finally, they crossed the state line into Colorado and Will breathed a sigh of relief. "We're home," he said.

"This is not what I expected Colorado to look like," she said.

"Just wait."

And she did until the Front Range came into view.

"Holy shit!" Jamie exclaimed. "I've seen pictures of this but I never imagined how beautiful it is, seeing it with my own eyes. Oh, Will, I'm so glad we came."

They spent the first night at his parents' house in

Lakewood. Bill Cain had reserved a rental house for them to check out just a few blocks from the Cain family home.

"It's a three-bedroom rancher," he explained to his son and Jamie. "If you don't like it, there's no obligation. You can look for something else. It might be okay until you can save enough money to buy or build a house of your own."

He gave them the address and they went to the house to check it out. "It's fine," Jamie assured Will, when she saw his nose turn up a bit.

"Are you sure?" he asked. "I'd hoped for something better for my wife and daughter.

"It's fine," she said again. "Let's get settled and then we can plan the future."

Will nodded. "I'm going to build you a house in Coal Creek Canyon. That's been my plan since I was in school."

"It's not necessary, Will."

"Yes, it is," he told her. "It's something I have to do."

"Okay, if that's what you want to do, but we can be happy in this house. We can be happy anywhere, as long as we're together."

"We'll rent the house, Dad," Will told his father. "When can I start to work?"

"I'd like you to take a business course at CU first," Bill said. "It's a two-month-long course, at night. You can work part time for that period. I don't want you too busy or too tired to give your full effort to the class. You don't need a degree, but this class will give you a lot of help on how to run a small business."

"Okay, Dad, thank you, but when do I start actually working?"

His dad chuckled. "You mean when do you start making money?"

Will smiled and nodded his head. "Yes, sir," he replied. "I don't want to waste time, I have a family to support."

"Yes, you do, son, and you've done well. The baby is just beautiful and your mother and I couldn't be more thrilled to have you back home again. I know you loved the navy, but I really think you made the right decision."

"I do too, Dad. When I saw the look in Jamie's eyes when the Front Range came in view, I knew I had made the right move."

"It won't be long before she'll feel like a native. Believe me. Colorado is addictive."

The class was not difficult for Will, not a lot of math, which had been his weakest subject in school, and it really did teach him a lot about running a business. As he slowly worked his way into one of the five stores his dad owned in Denver, Will began to meld the things he learned in class with the actual hands-on, day-to-day operation of the business. It soon became fun for him.

Jamie would quiz him about everything he did in his

job, and Will found himself rambling on and on about first one thing and then another. He'd tell her about a dissatisfied customer, who needed something the store didn't have, or a happy one, who came back to thank Bill for the advice he'd given on how to fix a sink or some household appliance.

It was a different world from what he'd been used to in the navy. There wasn't nearly as much profanity and none of the employees, who were mostly older men in their thirties and forties, had much to talk about except their kids and their home projects, or how the Broncos had done in last Sunday's game, which was typically not very good.

Long before the Denver Broncos became a successful football team they were often a source of embarrassment to the citizens of Denver and the state of Colorado. Denver had the worst record of any of the original AFL teams. They were the only team to have never played in a title game in the ten-year history of the league, and yet they had a passionate following in the city and the state. The loyal fan base was eventually rewarded for their patience, but in 1964 there was precious little for which they could cheer.

Will was not a great lover of football so, when his coworkers bemoaned the last Bronco loss, he just shook his head. "They'll get better one day."

Will began to see a side of his father that he'd hardly noticed when he was growing up. Bill was a very good businessman, and he ran his hardware "empire" with an easy efficiency that Will admired and sought to emulate. Bill made it look easy, but, as Will came to learn, it was *not* that easy. He began worrying about the day-to-day affairs more than he ought to and found that he was constantly running things through his mind at night. Sometimes he had difficulty going to sleep, due to continually worrying that he had missed something, forgotten something, or had done something wrong.

His dad saw the change in him and tried to calm him down. "It's not uncommon, son, what you're going through right now. You're afraid of messing up and you're stressing out about it. It will get better when you learn more about the business and feel more confident in your own abilities. Stop worrying. That's your primary mission now, stop worrying."

"It just seems so easy for you, Dad. I just can't keep everything in my head the way you do."

"I've been doing this for thirty years, Will. You can't expect to come in and do what I do right out of the gate. Relax, we have accountants to keep up with the money flow and good managers of the other stores. Once you've been here a while, it will start to fall into place for you."

In 1966, Jamie gave birth to a baby boy, whom they named Jamie, at Will's insistence and against the advice of almost everyone in the family, including the boy's mother. The confusion came later when the boy was older. Someone would call his name and his mother would answer. Conversely when Will would call to his wife, the baby boy would come to see what he wanted. Will finally conceded that, although his intentions were good, naming the boy after his mother had been a mistake, and the boy became "James" to his family and friends.

A year later, they had saved enough money to put down payment on a house. The owner of the house they were renting, a man named Frank Slayton, who was getting on up in years, offered to sell them the house they were living in. They decided to buy the house and fix it up. Will then started saving for the house he planned to build one day in Coal Creek Canyon.

Cain's Hardware started as one single store on Simms Street, just off Sixth Avenue, in Lakewood. It wasn't far from either of the Cain residences, so Will was spared, for the time being, from the heavy city traffic that made a working person's daily commute to and from work such a misery.

In time Bill added four additional stores—in Thornton, Aurora, Littleton, and, some years later, in Boulder. Bill and Ellen had gotten rich in the hardware business. Bill was a frugal man and unpretentious. He and his wife resisted the temptation to buy a bigger and better house. They remodeled and added rooms to the house to provide additional space as their children were born. Will was their first, then Julie and Thomas. The Cains loved their house and their neighborhood and just didn't want to leave. They were comfortable in this house they had bought when they were first married, and they sought to instill the same sense of frugality in their children.

Will, however, had dreamed of building a house in the mountains. As a boy, he developed a passion for Coal Creek Canyon, a passage through the mountains that was accessible by State Highway 72 out of Arvada or Lakewood. He had often camped in an area near the little community of Wondervu and that was where he had determined that, one day, he would build a home for his family.

Until that time arrived, Will busied himself with learning his father's hardware business. His brother Thomas, four years his junior, wanted no part of the hardware business. Thomas wanted to be a lawyer. Bill was not displeased with that. His firstborn son would take over the business one day and his youngest would be a lawyer. He could see the benefit of having a lawyer in the family.

Thomas ultimately decided to go to CU in Boulder. Will's sister Julie married a man from Pueblo whom she had met at a high school football game. The man was a Hispanic, named Joel Castillo, and he worked for a construction company that was based in Pueblo but did highway construction projects all over the state.

If Bill had any faults they were not easy to see, but his disdain for Hispanics, he made no effort to conceal. He'd agreed to walk his daughter down the aisle at her wedding, but his discomfort was more than apparent when he found the Catholic Church filled with Mexicans. Will acted as an emissary and ran interference for his father, meeting the parents and family of his new brother-in-law and trying to smooth over the obvious tension created by his father's bigotry.

"Nothing good ever came out of Pueblo," Bill said.

Julie moved to Pueblo with her husband and made frequent trips back home to see the family. When she gave birth to a baby girl, they named her Maria Ellen, after Joel's and Julie's mothers. Bill softened and asked Julie to start bringing her husband to the house with her when she came. The little girl was clearly a Latino, with dark eyes and hair like her father. Bill now had two granddaughters and a grandson and found himself warming up to the father of this new little girl, who looked at him with wide-eyed wonder and melted his heart.

Will began to forgive his dad for the older man's harsh stance in the early years of his sister's marriage. When he was growing up, Will had never fully realized the disdain in which his father had held Hispanic people. He'd had Hispanic friends when he was in school, and Bill had always treated them with respect.

Will supposed that his daughter's marriage to Joel Castillo brought out old prejudices Bill had held since his childhood. But when four-year-old Clare and one-year-old Maria Ellen sat on his lap, all that hidden bigotry went away, and he was just proud to be a grandpa to the two lovely sprites.

# CHAPTER 3

*Evan*

I love you, Evan." His grandmother hugged the boy and kissed his cheeks. "I love you more than anything in the world."

The five-year-old boy looked at her as if he didn't understand her, his big brown eyes staring intently into hers.

"Do you not understand what it means when I say, 'I love you?'"

The boy shook his head.

Emily Green had asked her daughter Faye, Evan's mother, many times why the boy never told her he loved her when she was continually assuring her grandson of her love for him. The answer was always the same.

Her husband's family was a strange breed of people, apparently from several generations back. George's parents never expressed their love to him verbally. George Garner lived his entire life under the misguided notion that one should "show" one's love for those he cared about rather than express shallow and superficial verbiage that served only to make another feel good. This was George's philosophy and he lived by it and demanded that his wife do the same.

"How in the world did you two ever get married?" Emily once asked her daughter, astonished that people could live that way. But when she kept her grandson on occasion, she continued to express her love for him with words and deeds. He was a genuinely loving and outgoing child and yet, to her sorrow, he only uttered, "I love you too, Grandma," one time in his life.

When Evan was seventeen years old and his grandmother was dying, she pulled him close to her and in a faintly audible voice said again, "I love you, Evan, my darling boy."

"I love you too, Grandma," he said and hugged her for the last time.

Tears filled his eyes as she passed away.

Evan was a popular kid in school, despite the stunted, emotion-denying values his father had passed on to him. He had an easy going way with girls and became sexually active by the time he was sixteen years old. He was honest, even when discretion demanded a bit of guile. He was a loyal friend and an uncompromising enemy. If a friend did him wrong, Evan never forgave and never forgot. He didn't practice revenge. He merely forgot that the person ever existed at all.

Girls found him caring and attentive and in possession of great sexual prowess in bed. His refusal to ever tell a girl he loved her was not of any great consternation in the free and easy crowd of high school in the early 1980s, but the occasional more devoted relationship-seeking girl found him to be superficial and pretentious, once they came to the conclusion that he was not a seriously romantic person.

Evan had a greater purpose in life, however, than the mere playing of musical beds with high school girls. His father, while not having instilled in him the greatest of human character traits, had convinced him of the importance of getting an education. The Garners were not wealthy people. They were not destitute, but life had been a struggle for George Garner, and he wanted better for his only child.

Evan made the honor roll in his freshman year in high school and remained there throughout his tenure, graduating with an A+ average and acing his Scholastic Achievement Test scores so well that he was offered an academic scholarship from the University of Colorado in Boulder. It was a godsend for Evan and even more so for George, who could scarcely afford to pay the full cost to send his son to college. As it was, Evan would have to work part time to fill in the personal expense gaps not covered by the scholarship.

He wanted to be a petroleum engineer. He'd read ads that offered big money for oversees work, which also provided great benefits and tax advantages. He had made up his mind that was what he wanted to do. He had made inquiries at several oil companies prior to beginning his first year of college and had received correspondence from a couple, advising him to keep them apprised of his progress and continued interest in pursuing his chosen field.

He fell in love with Boulder. He thought it was such a beautiful and eclectic town. Nestled right against the mountains, and with the five Flatiron rock formation stretching north and south along Green Mountain, Boulder had a unique identity all its own. Boulder Canyon, nearby, provided a quick and easy way to get into the mountains which he loved to do every chance he got.

Greeley was not a bad town to live in or to have grown up in, but Evan enjoyed being closer to the mountains. He enjoyed hunting and fishing, when he could afford it, and when he could find the time. He spent most nights in his dormitory room studying and preparing for tests. Occasionally, he went out at night with a couple of friends from the dormitory but, since Evan was not a drinker—he never drank more than two beers when he did drink—he was generally considered to be a good guy to take along as a designated driver. Evan could be counted on to keep his head if they were stopped by the police.

Evan had meticulously planned his life for the immediate foreseeable future. He would finish his four years at CU, get a job with a leading oil company, go overseas, and make his fortune. Then he would return to Colorado, build a house in the mountains, and live off his investments.

He really hadn't thought much farther out than that, had not imagined any need to contemplate any further pondering of what the future might have in store for him. He was faced with insurmountable opportunities, he thought, chuckling at an old joke he'd heard somewhere. But events sometimes had a way of intervening in the life of a young man with so much ambition, and it often happened in strange places and at times when least expected.

Life caught up with Evan one afternoon about halfway through his first semester at CU. He was sitting at a table in the Student Center, eating a sandwich and drinking a coke, when a blonde-haired girl sat down at the table across from him and plopped down her books. While she spread out her notebook paper and opened her books—preparing to study, he assumed—he watched her. She had shoulder-length hair that she kept partially clipped together in the back. She appeared to be about five feet, four inches tall and was slender but not skinny. He couldn't take his eyes off her, and he became worried that she would catch him staring at her, so he forced himself to look away. But he couldn't stop glancing back at her.

She looked up once, saw him looking at her, and smiled. He smiled back and she returned to her studying. He realized that he couldn't continue staring at her, and he thought it was too soon to go over and ask her out, so he got up and left, thinking he would come back tomorrow and force an introduction.

The next day, however, she was not there. "Dammit," he said to himself out loud, "I blew it."

Two subsequent visits to the Student Center failed to produce the beautiful blonde-haired girl. He wondered if he had dreamed her up, but was certain he had not, so, he determined that he would go back one more day. He went to sleep that night, dreaming of the blonde-haired girl. What was her name? Where was she from? What would it be like to kiss her? He was already imagining their first kiss. But what if she were not there tomorrow? What if she was just visiting from out of town and would never be here again? What would he do then?

He didn't know what he would do. He didn't want to imagine that.

She did a double-take when she saw him, as she sat down at the same table where she had been before. She smiled and gave a slight wave, with her free hand, that was not carrying books.

*She remembers me*, he thought. He was in unfamiliar

territory here. He was nervous. He'd never been nervous about approaching a member of the opposite sex before. He tried to appear nonchalant but it wasn't working for him. So, without belaboring the subject any longer, he stood up and walked over to her table.

She looked up and he saw that her eyes were bright blue. "Bluer than a robin's eggs," he noted, borrowing a line from the Joan Baez song. And her eyes were captivating, for they caught his eyes and he couldn't look away. She giggled when he told her he had been there every day for the last four days waiting to see her again. She told him to sit down, if he wanted to, and he did.

He asked her out and she said yes. He discovered that she was a local girl who lived with her family somewhere in the mountains, but she had an apartment in Boulder. She wrote down the address for him and gave him her phone number.

He called a couple of days later and asked her if she were free on Thursday night. "I know it's a little unusual to go out to dinner on a school night," he told her, "but there's this place up in the canyon in Nederland. It's an Italian restaurant with great food but it's small and very hard to get into on the weekend. If we go on Thursday, it won't be such a long wait."

She knew the place he was talking about but didn't want to tell him because she sensed that, he believed it was his special secret place, and she didn't want to burst his bubble. "Of course," she said. "Thursday works for me."

"I love the drive up through Boulder Canyon," he said, on the way up to Nederland. "I'm from Greeley, a flatlander, and I love the mountains."

"You'd like my dad, then. He was born and raised in Colorado and always had, like, this spiritual relationship with the mountains. He built us his dream house in Coal Creek Canyon. That's over near Golden."

"Are you originally from Colorado?" he asked her.

"I was actually born in Maine but my parents brought me here when I was five months-old."

"Maine? Wow, how did that happen?"

"My dad was in the navy, in a patrol squadron stationed in Brunswick, Maine. That's where he met my mother. They had me right before he got out, and they brought me home to Colorado. So, I am basically a native."

"That's good enough for me," he said, and she smiled, nodding her head.

When they pulled into the parking lot at Neapolitans she tried to act as if she'd never been there. But that act was foiled as soon as the waitress came to the table.

"Hello, Evan," she said, "Good to see you again. Hey, Clare, I haven't seen you around for a while. How's your family? Tell that good-looking brother of yours to come and see me."

They made small talk for a few minutes and then ordered their food.

Evan looked at her and smiled. "Thank you," he said.

"For what?"

"For trying to let me think I was taking you to some new and exciting place you'd never been before."

"That's okay. Our house is in Coal Creek canyon which is down the road the other way out of town. My dad brings us here every so often. It was cool that you thought of bringing me here."

They finished their meal and the waitress brought the check. "I had no idea that you two were an item, Evan," she said.

"I didn't either until two days ago, Genna," he replied.

Genna smiled at Clare and Clare smiled at Evan.

The sun was starting to go down and he turned the car off the road and into a space on the shore of the lake. "Let's watch the sun set on the water, okay?"

"Sure," she said. They both sat there staring at the shimmering slithers of sunlight dancing on the blue water of Barker Resevoir. "Are you going to kiss me?" she asked him.

"I was thinking about it."

She slid across the seat right up next to him. "Well think a little faster," she said.

Evan laughed and put his arm around her. Their lips met. It was a cataclysmic moment for both of them. They couldn't stop. Finally, it was he who broke away from her. He stared deeply into her eyes, and they both knew that something magical and wonderful had just happened between them.

"I may need a paramedic if we don't stop this," he said.

She started giggling and was still giggling when he drove back onto the highway.

They started going out regularly, but more often than not, they hung out at her apartment and watched movies. She made sandwiches or hamburgers. She realized that he was not well off, so she didn't insist on going out to eat.

She took him home with her, for the weekend, to meet her family and Evan was well accepted. To her mild disappointment, he and her brother James became immediate friends. They would eventually become best friends and spend days at a time, traveling deep into the mountains, hunting and fishing.

"I think Evan likes James more than he likes me," she told her mother.

"Not hardly, Clare," her mother replied. "I've seen the way he looks at you. The boy is smitten."

"I hope so, Mom, I really hope so."

"Trust me on this. I know that look."

Evan was indeed in love with Clare, and he showed it. He showered her with attention, not clinging attention but the kind of attention that said to her that she was the only girl in the world, as far as he was concerned. He wanted desperately to make love to her but he had determined that he was not going to press the issue. He dreamed about it at night, imagined what it would be like. It was almost as if he had convinced himself that it had already happened. But he would not suggest it nor would he even hint that he wanted to get her in bed.

He didn't have to, as it turned out. They had been studying late one night at her place and she asked him to stay the night.

Despite his excitement at her offer, he remained perfectly calm and in control of himself. She was nervous, undressed quickly, and jumped into bed and under the covers even more quickly. Nevertheless, he managed to catch a glimpse of her naked body as she made her move to secret herself beneath the covers.

"Dear God," he said out loud, and then thought. *She's so beautiful.* He'd never seen such a beautiful woman, not in all his life.

Their lives were not the same after that. They became inseparable, always holding hands when they walked together, always embracing with their heads leaning against each other's. They were the perfect picture of a couple head over heels in love. Clare was verbal with her love, constantly telling him she loved him.

"I'm crazy about you too, baby," he often responded, leaving her with a nagging sense that something was missing.

Her mother tried to help but was of little comfort to

her. "Some men just have a hard time saying that phrase, dear."

"But Daddy is not like that, is he?"

"No, he isn't. Most men are easy with it. Evan may be struggling with issues from his childhood. Maybe his parents didn't express their love for him the way our family did, and does, for each other."

"I just hope he gets out of it at some point in our lives." Clare said, just a bit dejectedly.

When they graduated in 1986, Evan left for the job he had been offered in Indonesia. He asked her to wait for him and she said she would. He wanted to build them a house when he returned. He left her standing at the gate, at Stapleton Airport, feeling like the only man she would ever love might not ever come back to her.

# CHAPTER 4

*The House in Coal Creek Canyon*

Over the years, Will came to appreciate, and gain much respect for, his father's business acumen. Bill simply had a head for business. He carried around in his head most of the necessary information that was needed to keep the hardware stores operating smoothly and profitably. He had taught Will the business more quickly than Will had ever thought possible. It had been hard work and long hours but it had paid off. In 1970, he was made assistant manager of the entire operation, working directly under his dad.

Bill was fifty-six years old, still a relatively young man, but he had an eye on the future and a time when he would no longer be able to run his business. He wanted his son to be ready to take over and not have a learning curve to deal with.

Bill's health, however, was slowly failing, so in 1973, he began to take a reduced role in the day-to-day operations. He let Will take over for him as general manager.

The job was stressful for Will, but he found the hours more flexible. He had managers over each store, so he didn't absolutely have to be there at the crack of dawn every day. He usually was on the job early but he didn't have to be. His salary had gone up substantially, and with profit sharing and bonuses and increased salary, they were making good money.

One Saturday he told his wife to gather the kids together and get them in the car. They were going on a day-trip. Jamie called the two children, nine-year-old Clare and seven-year-old James, and ushered them into the car. Will backed out of the driveway and headed out toward the mountains.

"Where are we going, Daddy?" Clare asked him.

"We're going to see where our new home is going to be, baby," he told her.

"So, you're finally going to do it?" his wife said.

"Yep, it's time. I'm not getting any younger. I promised to build you a home in the mountains, and I'm going to do it."

He drove up Highway 72 into Coal Creek Canyon.

"This is the canyon I told you about, where I used to go camping with my dog, Boxer."

Jamie was enthralled with looking at the forest and, every so often, she could catch a glimpse of the mountains through the trees and rocks. 'It's beautiful, Will," she said.

'We'll be coming up on a little community called Wondervu—yeah, it's misspelled, you will undoubtedly notice when you see the sign but nobody cares. I put a down payment on a couple of acres high up on a rise above the road about a mile or so past Signal Rock Road. The house will overlook the highway and will be tiered, that is multi-layered, so to speak to speak, to fit the contour of the terrain.

He drove up to the property and they all got out to look around. He motioned for them to follow him around to the other side of the lot. "From the edge of the bluff, where the back of the house will be, we'll be able to sit on our patio and watch the sun go down over the Front Range and the Arapaho National Forest."

"Oh, Will, it's so beautiful," Jamie said. "Thank you. I can't wait until the house is built."

"It'll take a few months, they'll have to construct a staging area and build a road up to the location. There will be one switchback but not too much of a climb. It might be a little scary in winter, but for a girl who grew up in Maine, it shouldn't be too much trouble navigating in and out of the canyon."

"How much is it going to cost, Will?

"Back on the ground it would cost about forty-thousand, but up here in the sky, we'll add about twenty to that."

"Wow," she said, her eyebrows raising. "Can we afford that?"

"Yes, we can, darling. We're doing okay."

"I guess I married well," Jamie said, smiling at him.

"You married beneath your station, beautiful. I'm the one who hit the jackpot." He took her in his arms and kissed her, long and passionately, and she returned his desire. They didn't stop until they noticed the children giggling.

"Now what are you laughing about, Clare bear?" Will asked his daughter.

"You were kissing Mommy, Daddy," the girl said.

"We are happy, baby. We're going to be moving into a brand-new house in a few months. Do you think you'll like it here?"

She nodded her head.

"I'll like it here too, Daddy," seven-year old James chipped in.

"Well, I hope so buddy, because you and I are going to go camping a lot when we get moved in, just the two of us. Would you like that?"

A loud "Yes" came out of the boy, and Clare demanded that she be able to go camping with them.

"Camping is not for girls," her brother told her.

"Oh, come on, James," Will said. "We can take Clare with us sometimes, can't we?"

The boy reluctantly nodded his head.

Will had decided to act as the general contractor for the construction of the house to save the percentage that a builder would charge. Before it was finished, he had come to wish he'd paid the extra money. Coordinating all the trades, especially given the remote location, proved to be an arduous task.

The electricians had installed a temporary power pole on the job, so Will rented a small travel trailer and started spending some nights at the site. He figured it would save some time, getting the trades coordinated in the mornings, before he left to go to work. Jamie came with him one night and that was enough for her. His wife was not into deprivation and austerity. Her idea of "roughing it" was staying at a Motel 6. So, he 'bit the bullet' and continued the grueling task of getting his house built.

Surprisingly, the house was finished a month earlier than he had anticipated but the guest house was not completed until after they had already moved in. As soon as the guest house was finished, Jamie's parents came to visit for a week. Will had added the guest house primarily with the Dunhams in mind. It had a small kitchenette, a nice size living room, and a bedroom loft that looked out over the mountains.

Jamie home-schooled the children until they were

ready for middle school, then they were enrolled in a school in Golden. She had to drive them every day, so Will bought a four-wheel drive Jeep, to help her get up and down the canyon more easily in rough weather.

At sixteen, Clare started her freshman year at Golden High School in Golden, which was easily accessible by going down the canyon road and taking Highway 93 right to the school. Her brother would follow her just two years later. Their mother would drive them to school every morning and pick them up every afternoon.

Sixteen-year-old Clare was a younger version of her mother, the same height at five feet, four inches and almost the same slender build. Although her mother outweighed her by a few pounds, it was noticeable only by the bathroom scale. Jamie, just twenty-one years older than her daughter still turned heads wherever she went. Clare, it appeared, was going to be no less a magnet to the opposite sex. She was constantly being sought after by one boy or another. She dated on occasion but, by her senior year, had not yet entered into a serious relationship.

When her brother joined her at GHS, he took it upon himself to act as her protector. If a boy seemed to be making a nuisance of himself around his sister, James would advise the boy to buzz off, although he typically used a fouler term. Occasionally, Clare would have to tell him to lay off a boy, in whom she had taken an interest.

One boy took a shine to Clare and was persistent

enough to eventually convince her to at least "give him the time of day." Jimmy Baxter was the son of a well-to-do family that attended the same church to which the Cains belonged, Standley Lake Methodist Church on Eighty-Sixth Parkway in Westminster.

Jimmy had "fallen" for Clare when the Cains first started going to the church, when the two of them were fourteen years old. But Jimmy's love for the blonde-haired beauty was an unrequited love, for she showed little interest in him until they were both in high school. She then agreed to go out with him on occasion. They dated on and off through their senior year. He asked her to go to the prom with him. Another boy had asked her as well and she considered going with him, instead but reconsidered after a talk with her mother.

"You don't want to toy with a boy's affections, dear," Jamie told her. "It's just not right and it might make people think you're petty and vindictive. If you don't want to go to the prom with Jimmy, then tell him that, but don't go with another boy just to taunt him. You just never know how a boy will react to something like that."

"But he's such a nerd, Mother."

"What about the other boy who asked you, what's he like?"

"He's on the football team," Clare said.

"Do you like him?"

"No, not really. He's okay but he's kind of goofy acting. I think he just wants to get in my pants."

"Oh, then let's not go to the prom with him."

"Okay, Mother, I guess I'll have mercy on Jimmy Baxter and go with him. It's the least I can do."

"Oh, my, the perils facing a young man enamored with Clare Cain must be overwhelming. I hope you don't ruin this boy's life."

Clare stuck her tongue out at her mother and stomped out of the room.

She was bored to death at the prom with Jimmy, but she tried to make the best of it. He took her "parking'" after the dance and she perceived that he wanted to kiss her.

She allowed him a couple of lip encounters until she realized he was becoming aroused.

"All right, Jimmy, back off," she said, and slid back over to the other side of the car.

Jimmy told her he was in love with her, and she told him that she did not share those same feelings for him. He became angry at first and then conciliatory, hoping to win her over with kind treatment and proper behavior. "But I do love you, Clare," he said. "I've loved you since the first time I saw you. Just give me a chance."

"I can't make myself feel something I don't, Jimmy."

"I just wish you'd try, I want to marry you."

"Marry me? Oh, for crap's sake, Jimmy, we just got

out of high school, I'm not going to think about getting married now, not for a long time yet."

"No, I don't mean now," he said, frustrated. "I mean after college. I'm going to Harvard in the fall and then to law school. Just tell me you'll think about it. That's all I'm asking you."

"Okay, Jimmy, I'll think about it."

For the time being, that was sufficient for Jimmy to sustain his hope for the future. He was smiling all the way back to Clare's house to drop her off. He wanted to kiss her goodnight before she got out of the car, and she consented. But when he put his hand on her breast, she slapped him.

"You asshole," she said. "I said I'd think about it. That doesn't give you groping privileges."

Jimmy apologized profusely and begged her forgiveness. She told him to forget it. She got out of his car and he started to get out to walk her to the door but she yelled at him. "Stay put, I can find my way to the door."

Clare was slowly becoming aware of just how attractive she was to members of the opposite sex. She was continually being told how pretty she was and boys were always flirting with her. But her father and her brother treated her like one of the guys. They took her camping with them on occasion and never cut her any slack when it came to the work load. She eventually learned that fathers and brothers looked at their daughters and sisters with different eyes, than did normal young male animals they encountered in their daily lives. Clare was an astonishingly beautiful female creature, and she was the last one to fully realize just how stunning she was.

When Clare decided to go to CU, she knew she wouldn't have to see Jimmy Baxter again for a long time. When she met Evan Garner, she forgot that Jimmy had ever existed. Evan made her understand who and what she was and what sort of feelings she could create deep inside a man just by walking into his view.

The house, that her dad had built for them in Coal Creek Canyon, had become a place of so much joy to Clare, and to the entire Cain family, that she almost could not conceive of ever living anywhere else. She assumed that, when Evan returned from overseas, they would get married and live in a house that he built for them. Hopefully, they would have children and their house would become like the loving home in which she had grown up.

In 1987, Bill's health took a turn for the worse and he was not expected to live much longer. Will, and his sister Julie, and brother Thomas, decided it would be best to move their parents into the guest house at Will's house in Coal Creek Canyon where their father could be better taken care of. They made the move in early '88 after the family had returned from their Christmas vacation in Maine.

It was a bittersweet time for Clare and her brother James. They dearly loved their grandparents on both sides of the family, but to watch Bill slowly dying was torture to them. The man who literally had made possible everything they had, materially and inspirationally in the world, had always been so full of life and energy. This was not taking anything away from their father, who had worked hard and earned everything they had, but it was their grandfather who had given him the opportunity. Now they could only try to make what time he had left with them as comfortable and as enjoyable as possible.

Most evenings Bill liked to sit on the back patio and watch the sun go down over the mountains. Jamie would bring him coffee and cinnamon rolls or some other of his favorite pastries and Will would often join him if he could get away from the office early enough.

"How's it going, Dad?" Will said, patting him on his arm.

"I love the sunshine on the mountains in the after-noon." His words came slowly now.

"I do, too," Will replied, "that's why I put the back of the house facing west."

"You always did love this canyon, even when you were just a boy. I never really understood it until now. I just loved to hunt and fish, didn't really care where. What I mean is I never really noticed how beautiful the mountains and the forests are, I just wanted to shoot some-thing." Bill was out of breath and struggling to finish his sentences.

"Take your time, Pop. We've got plenty of time. You want some more coffee?"

Bill nodded his head.

Will picked up his cup, went into the kitchen, and returned a minute later with a fresh cup. He sat it down on the table in front of his dad, and Bill just smiled.

Will pulled his chair closer to his dad and motioned to him that he wanted to talk. "Dad, I have something I want to say to you. I know I've thanked you for all you've done for me. But I have to tell you again how grateful I am, how grateful we all are, for you talking me into coming into the business with you. I owe everything to you and I can never repay it—and I know, you're shaking your head. I know what you're going to say, but I do owe you for everything I have been able to do and have, Dad. I didn't pay much attention to what you did when I was growing up but I have to say this, if I knew half of what you know, I'd know twice what I do. I love you, Pop, and I've waited way too long to tell you that."

There were tears in his dad's eyes. He reached for Will's hand, squeezed it, and nodded. Will stood up, leaned over the chair, hugged his dad, and patted him on his head.

Bill died in November of 1988. He was seventy-one-years-old.

Bill wanted Will's sister Julie and her family to have the house in Lakewood and the profits from one of the hardware stores. Will would decide which one. Thomas, being the company lawyer would receive a retainer and then would charge the business for any legal work performed on its behalf. Everything else would be Will's, and he would, of course, manage the business as he deemed wise and proper.

Will contemplated adding additional stores across the state but ultimately decided against it because he just didn't want to expand farther than he could keep a tight control on things. "Don't let your reach extend beyond your grasp...or something like that," his dad always said.

# CHAPTER 5

## *Working Girl*

C lare began receiving job offers from various firms around the area but, in October, her interest was drawn to a letter from the City of Denver, requesting that she come in for an interview for a job in societal research, something about which she knew absolutely nothing. She decided to check it out, so she called and made an appointment.

Luckily, the city and county office building had a parking garage, because Denver traffic was horrendous and finding a parking space was a living nightmare. Clare took her ticket with her to get it validated and found the office number where they had told her to report. She took the elevator to the second floor and, looking at her hand-written note to double check her memory, she found Room 214, opened the door, and walked into the reception area.

An elderly woman at the reception desk was on the phone. She looked up at Clare and held up her index finger on her left hand to signal for her to wait a moment. When she was finished, she smiled at Clare. "Can I help you, Miss?"

"My name is Clare Cain and I have an appointment with Mister Harvey," she said.

"Oh, right, he's expecting you, have a seat, darlin', and I'll let him know you're here."

A few minutes later, a tall dark-haired man, who appeared to be about her dad's age, came out of a door on the other side of the room. He walked toward Clare. "Miss Cain, I presume," he said.

"Yes, sir, Clare Cain."

"Okay, Miss Cain, come with me." He held the door for her and then led her down a hall to his office. "Have a seat," he said, pulling the chair out for her to sit down.

He asked for her diploma and her resume, and she handed them to him. He studied her credentials for a moment and then nodded his head. "Very good, Miss Cain, may I call you Clare?"

"Yes, sir, of course," she said.

"Good. Okay then, Clare, what we have in mind for you is a city-wide study we are initiating. The study will be to determine the benefits that City of Denver Parks and Recreation services have had on the individual neighborhoods in the past twenty-five years. We'll provide up-to-date data on when each city park was built and when other city neighborhood services were put into operation. Your job will be to conduct interviews throughout the city to gauge the impact, positive or negative, these services have had on the people in the neighborhoods. Does that sound like something you might be interested in doing?"

"My first thought is, Mister Harvey, that it sounds overwhelming but I'd like to see the data you spoke of so I can get a better idea of just what the job entails. I don't want to accept the job and then discover later that I can't handle it."

"That makes perfect sense, Clare, but I wouldn't be too concerned. We've allotted a year for the study and we'll get you two staffers. They'll be interns, two kids with some college experience but not graduates. You'll have a city car and a salary of thirty-K a year with benefits. There'll be a learning curve but I have no doubt you can do the job. I will help you out until you get a grip on things. So, what do you say?

Clare swallowed hard, when she heard the thirty-K salary, but she maintained her composure. "I'll take the job. Thank you for your confidence in me, Mister Harvey."

Clare was elated and rushed home to tell her parents,

who sat and listened attentively to her as she described with great animation what she would be doing in her job and how much money she would be making. She was especially happy about the money.

"I had no idea, Daddy, that I'd be making that much money. And I'll have a city car to drive so I won't have to put miles on my own car. I won't be able to drive it home, I can only use it when I'm working but it's really cool. I'm really happy."

"And I'm happy for you, baby," Will said, as he hugged her, "I know your mother is, too. But you need to develop a savings plan. You don't want to waste this opportunity by foolishly spending all your money."

"I won't," she insisted, "I want to have a lot of money saved up for when Evan gets back. He's socking his money away to build us a house and I want to help, too. But I want to help with the household expenses here, too, I want to pay rent."

"No, that won't be necessary, darling," her dad told her, and Jamie agreed. "We don't want you to do that. You save your money for when you get married."

Clare relented and promised them that she would be frugal with her newly acquired potential windfall. She was now looking forward to doing the job, and she was slowly losing the doubts she first had. She could do it, she knew she could.

When she received her business cards it was a rush of pride for her like she'd never experienced before.

*Clare Cain*
*Director of Research Services*
*City of Denver, Colorado*
*303-555-7348*

Her office was like a small conference room with two smaller rooms off to either side. Her two assistants would work out of these rooms. She discovered that she would be interviewing for the individuals who would work for her as her assistances. She had not been ready for that, assuming that they were already employed by the city. But she accepted the challenge.

Not being sure exactly how to proceed, Clare did what she always did in situations like the one in which she now found herself. She talked to her daddy. Will schooled his daughter on how to interview people and gave her some pointers on reading body language, facial expressions, and the like. He made her a list of typical questions to ask, reminding her that she would have to craft other questions that were more specific to the job the applicants would be expected to do. When she ran the ad in the paper and started taking calls and setting appointments, she felt more confident that she was up to the task that lay before her.

After a week of interviews, Clare decided to offer two individuals the jobs. She presented her decision to Nelson Harvey. He approved them and she made the calls. She hired a young man named Alex Peterson. Alex reminded Clare of her brother, except that James was taller, heavier, and more stoutly built. James was also better looking. Alex was about five feet, ten inches; weighed around one hundred fifty pounds, and had brown hair like James.

Martha Meacham, who went by Marty, was a plumpish girl about the same height as Clare. Very intelligent, Clare perceived from the interview, and congenial. Both kids were two years younger than Clare but both seemed capable of doing what she would need them to do.

They would begin by canvassing every city park in the city. Clare sent a memo to the Records Department, which was in the basement, requesting a set of chronological maps of all the city parks, pools, and other public facilities, showing the dates they were constructed and made available for public use.

When she received notification that the maps were ready for pickup, she took the elevator down to the basement and went to the window marked "Maps." A heavyset balding man approached the window. Upon seeing Clare standing there, he started licking his lips in a very lascivious and leering manner. It made her feel uncomfortable but she gave no indication that it had.

"Well, hello, gorgeous," the man said, winking at her, "what can I do for you?"

She stated her business, curtly without acknowledging that she'd even heard him.

"Well, don't be so stuck up, sweet-pants. I'll get

your maps for you. Come on back. You can help me find them."

"I'll wait here, thank you," she said.

"Suit yourself, doll. You don't have to get so huffy. I was just kidding with you."

"Your conversation is inappropriate, sir," Clare told him, "and I don't appreciate it."

With that the man left the window and returned about ten minutes later with several rolls of maps which he handed to Clare without speaking. She left the room and decided that the next time she needed something from the basement she would ask Alex to go pick it up.

This was not the first-time Clare would experience sexual harassment in the workplace. She came to learn that old habits and attitudes changed slowly and a suit-and-tie-corporate environment was not much safer for a woman than the assault of an uncouth and disrespectful man on a construction site.

She had become accustomed to the occasional whistle, or rude comment, on the street, in public, even on the enlightened and genteel campus of the staid University of Colorado. But to be verbally humiliated in the city and county municipal building of Denver, she was not ready for, and the incident left her shaken and disappointed. She told her family, and her mother offered some comfort, telling her that she had handled the situation exactly as she should have. Her father told her to report it to her supervisor.

"I really don't want to do that, Daddy. I'm new to the job and, if I report it, I might be perceived as a trouble-maker."

Her brother James offered a more practical and direct solution. "Tell me the guy's name, and I'll go in there and kick his ass."

She smiled, but shook her head. "You'll get in trouble if you do that."

"I don't care," he said.

"But I do," she replied. "I don't want you to do that, I'll handle it. If it happens again, I'll report it, I promise."

When the job started in earnest, Clare found that she really enjoyed the work. Alex and Marty turned out to be very capable and worked well with people. Many were more than willing to answer the questions the three city employees sought to ask them. But many others were inherently distrustful of authority so it was impossible to get a complete and full consensus.

Typically, they asked how long the person had lived in the neighborhood, how often they and their family used the facility, did they feel the facility was safe for their family and, if not, what improvements might be made that would make it safer. After six months of aggressive canvassing, Clare was beginning to see the possibility of being able to put together a comprehensive report that would satisfy the intent of the department.

She started getting letters from Evan about once a week, once they started coming. He had been out of her life for almost a year now and she still thought about him every day. Some of his letters were romantic, speaking only about the two of them and how much he missed her. Mainly, though, they were mechanical and business-like, telling her about his plans for the house he was going to build for them and how much money he'd saved toward that goal.

He used a lot of his letters to tell her about his job and the place he was working, how beautiful it was, and how primitive. They lived well on the Oil Company's facility but outside the compound it was a miserable place for the locals.

She answered every letter as soon as she received it. It seemed petty to tell him about her job when measuring it up against his. It just didn't seem that important.

She had completed a year of employment in October of '87 and was eligible for a one-week vacation. The project was not yet complete so Mister Harvey gave her a six-month extension to complete it, having seen her progress so far and being impressed with the results to date. The family was planning a trip back to Maine, at Christmas, to visit her mother's parents, and they wanted Clare to go with them. She applied for her one-week at that time and it was approved.

In April of 1988, Evan's letters stopped coming. When she had not received a letter by the first week of May, she called his parents and they told her the same thing—no word from Evan. She drove to Greeley one weekend to see them. They had called the company but could get no word on his situation. They seemed evasive to George Garner. Both parents were clearly worried. Clare suggested they contact the State Department and they told her they would do that and keep her informed.

In the meantime, she and her two faithful assistants had completed all the research. Now all that remained of the project was for Clare to compile the information into a comprehensive report of her findings that the city planners could use to determine what new facilities they might wish to propose to the city council for future development.

Alex and Marty would be relocating to a different department for the time being while Clare finished up the project. Clare took them to lunch to celebrate completion of the project. They went to a small bistro near the municipal building that was very popular with the lunchtime crowd. They clinked their glasses together in a toast.

"Good job, guys," Clare said. "I've really enjoyed working with you both."

"It was our pleasure," Marty said, looking at Alex who was nodding in agreement.

"Thank you, Marty, you two made the job easy—scratch that, you made it possible for me. I couldn't have done it without you. Seriously, I mean that."

"When is, your guy coming back, Clare?" Alex asked her.

"I don't know. He is supposed to be back in October

but we haven't heard from him. The company won't tell us anything and the government is being evasive."

"Damn, I had no idea. You must be terrified," Marty said.

"I am, I'm about to lose my mind, and his parents are distraught. I don't really know what to do."

"If there's anything we can do, just let us know."

"Thank you, guys," Clare said, "I appreciate it.

It became a waiting game for Clare. The longer the time span in which she received no word from Evan, the more frustrated she became. She missed him terribly, she missed having him around. She missed making love with him. She had to face facts. She was just plain horny. She chuckled when she described herself thusly, thinking it was something her brother would say.

She would never consider jumping into bed with some man just to alleviate a temporary condition, but she found herself reliving her last night with Evan before he flew out of her life. It almost made her dizzy when she thought about it…

e/ɔe/ɔ

Evan had rented a motel room and asked Clare to stay with him, one last time, before they were separated for two long years. Clare told her mother she was going to see Evan, at his folks' house before he left in the morning.

It was only a little fib, she told herself. Her mother just hugged her and told her to be careful.

When Clare walked out of the house, in her black strapless party dress, her mother was glad that Will was not home from work yet. She would make up a story for him later, and it would be just a little fib too.

Clare met Evan at the motel and, after he took her hand and helped her out of her car, they walked to the room. As he closed the door to the room he took her in his arms, put his hand on the side of her neck under her hair, pulled her face close to his, and kissed her. Evan had always been a good kisser but, this time, he was more intense than ever before. He kissed her tenderly, softly. She relaxed, went limp in his arms, and was eager to let him have his way with her. She was longing to hear him say, he loved, her but this time his kisses said it quite clearly.

"Let me look at you, baby. You're so beautiful, I can't believe you fell in love with me."

"I can't believe you fell in love with me, either," she whispered.

"It was the easiest thing I've ever done, Clare."

She unzipped her dress and let it fall to the floor then unsnapped her bra and let it fall. He caressed her shoulders, turned her around, and kissed them. He kissed her across her back as he gently fondled her breasts. Lifting her hair, he kissed her neck as she leaned back against him and uttered a low moan from deep within her.

"You are so beautiful," he whispered in her ear."

"You said that already."

"I did?"

"Yes, but that's okay," she said.

He picked her up, carried her to the bed, lay her down, and slowly took off her panties. He looked into her eyes, as he did it, and they smiled at each other.

Then he undressed himself while she watched him. She reached for his hand and pulled him to her as he got into the bed. He held her and caressed her like they'd been in love forever. She heard a faint voice, like it was coming from somewhere else, saying his name, over and over, telling him he was fantastic, and how good he was, and how he made her feel. She suddenly realized it was her own voice she was hearing. The voice continued and she could not silence it.

She heard herself whimper and make noises like she had not made when they had made love before. This time it was different, even better, if possible, than all the times before. She clutched at him and dug her fingernails into his back. She let out a cry, almost a scream but not a scream, more of a gasp as he gave her the one thing she so desperately needed.

When it was over, he put his arms around her, pulled her over next to him, and kissed her again with the same passion. She then laid her head on his chest and put her arm around his midsection. They lay there until she thought she might fall asleep, then he spoke to her.

"I don't know how we are going to get through these next two years, baby, but I promise you that, if you will wait for me, I will never do this again. When I come back from Indonesia, I'll build us that house and I'll get some other job if necessary but I'll never leave you again."

"I'll wait for you, Evan. It's not going to be easy but it will be a lot easier for me than it will for you. I hate what you are going to have to do but I know you're doing it for us and I love you for it."

I want to have a girl first just like your folks did. I want a girl who looks just like you."

"Well, yes, sir," she said and saluted, "your baby-making machine is at your disposal."

"Hold that thought until I get back."

"Don't worry, I will." She said.

"Listen, Clare, you're a beautiful woman. The first time I saw you without your clothes I almost swallowed my tongue."

"You did not."

"I did too, anyway, what I was going to say was, lots of men are going to be after you, wanting you. Please wait for me and I promise I will be good to you."

'You already are good to me, Evan. You can't be any better."

"Just don't forget me, please, Clare, don't forget me.

"I'll never forget you Evan Garner, I love you, you ought to know that by now."

❧❧❧

Whenever she got really depressed, and missing Evan, she would go to her room, turn off the light, and lie on her bed, thinking about their last night together. It was what sustained her, it was all that sustained her during this awful time in her life.

It had been months now since she had gotten a letter from Evan. Her mind raced with the possibilities of what could have happened to him, and none of the possibilities were good. At a time when she needed to be concentrating on her job and planning on Evan's return and their future together, she was terrified that she might not ever see him again.

She talked to the Garners every other day or so and went to Greeley at least once a month but they were as distraught as she was, if not more so. There was still no news coming from the company or from the US State Department.

They had simply cut off all lines of communications with the families of AOE employees. As maddening as it was for Clare and the Garners, there was really nothing they could do but wait. She even imagined that something had happened to the mail system in the remote location in Indonesia where Evan was working but quickly decided that made no sense. The company would have informed them because they would have been in contact with him. It was much more serious than that. Something had happened and, for some unknown reason, they didn't want to tell them what it was. It was either that, or they didn't know what had happened to them.

# CHAPTER 6

*Brunswick*

*Christmas 1987:*

Their plane landed at Portland airport, and after they off loaded and retrieved their baggage, Will rented a car for the drive to Brunswick. They arrived at the Dunham's house on Federal Street, and Richard and June were standing in the yard waiting for them. June went to hug her daughter first and then the two grandkids, Clare and James.

"Oh, my goodness, look at you two," June said. "You're twice as big as you were the last time we saw you."

"Hi, Grandma," James said. He hugged June and shook hands with Richard Dunham. "Good to see you again, Grandpa."

"I'm so glad to see you all," Richard said. "I was afraid you and Clare might not come."

"I'll always come to see you and Grandma, when Mom and Dad come back to Maine," James said. "I love to come here."

After all the congenialities and formalities were made, they all settled into their designated spaces then gathered in the living room to talk over old times and new times.

June made dinner for them, and they all ate their fill. Richard and his grandson, James, wanted to go hunting but deer season was over so they decided to go to Richard's hunting camp, drink beer, and shoot their guns.

"Boys will be boys," June said. "You'd better not get my grandson drunk or shot, Richard Dunham."

"I'll take care of the boy, June, stop worrying," he told her.

Will and Jamie were going down to Bailey Island, like they did every time they returned to Maine, to relive the days when they first met. Clare would stay with Grandma June and listen to stories about when her mother was a little girl.

The trips back to Maine always evoked much nostalgia in both Will and Jamie. It was where they met and fell in love, got married, and had a baby girl. It represented so much to them that they always felt an onset of sadness when it was time to leave again. They passed the parish church, where they were married, and drove past the old naval air station which was still operational, although VP-21 had been decommissioned in 1969.

They headed down Highway 24 toward Bailey Island to relive again one of their many forays down to Land's End, where they first realized they were in love. They sat on the rocks there and stared out into Casco Bay for at least an hour. They made out like teenagers and then laughed about it.

"Married twenty-three years and I still love you just as much as I did the first time we came here, Jamie," Will said.

"I do too, darling. I love you too just as much."

"Are you sorry we left?"

"No," was all she said.

She seemed to be in deep thought so Will just looked at her and left her to her thoughts.

Jamie's mind drifted back in time to the carefree days when they first met...

ᘒᘓᘒ

*February 1961*:

"You're Sam's friend, aren't you?" she asked him.

Will nodded. "We're crewmates."

"So, what's your name, so I don't have to say, hey you?"

"Cain, William Joseph," he told her, "but I go by Will."

"So, formal," she said, smiling at him. "Well I'm Dunham, Jamie Lynn, and I go by Jamie." She held out her hand. He took it and they shook hands. "So, you're a flyer?" she asked.

"More of a rider," he said. "I'm the electrician on our crew."

"Sam still comes into J and J but I was expecting to see you with him. Where have you been?" she asked.

"Well, you told Sam that your dad didn't let you date navy guys, so I figured I'd save myself a broken heart and just never see you again."

"Oh, so you're a fatalist," she said.

"I'm not sure what that means."

"It means that you accept whatever fate comes your way. I did smile at you, I thought that was enough to at least let you know I thought you were cute."

"You think I'm cute?" he said.

"Yes, I think you're cute, do you think I'm cute? I mean, you did smile back at me."

"No, I think you're beautiful," he said.

She smiled at him and looked right into his eyes. "Then why didn't you come and tell me that?"

He sighed. "I don't know why, I just couldn't."

"Fear of rejection, isn't it?" she said.

"Yes, it's a character flaw, I suppose."

"So where do we go from here?" she asked.

"Will you go out with me?"

"If my dad says it's okay, I will. You'll have to come to the house, maybe for dinner, one night and meet my parents. Are you up for that?"

"Sure," he said. "Does your father own any guns?"

"He does but he won't shoot you," she said. "I won't let him."

⁓⁓⁓

"So how do I get to Bailey Island?" he asked her as they pulled away from her house.

"Go like you were going back to the base, but go past the base and stay on highway twenty-four all the way down. I usually have lunch with my dad on Saturdays but I begged off this morning to go with you."

"I hope he doesn't blame me for that. We could have gone later."

"It's okay," she said, "I want you to see a part of Maine that you've never seen."

"I've flown over quite a bit of it, and I went to Lewiston once with Andy Malik and Egg Money."

"Egg Money?" she said, looking at him inquisitively.

"Oh, yeah, Jimmy Watson, the radioman on my crew." He told her how Jimmy had come by the name and that Andy was another crewmate who was from

Lewiston and still went home occasionally on weekends.

"Egg Money, oh—kay," she said. "What do they call you?"

"Will, usually, and some other names I can't repeat. Officially, everyone goes by their last name. I mean, the Officers and Chiefs call us by our last names, but most of the riff raff call each other by their first names or whatever nickname that might apply."

"We are on Orr's Island now," Jamie said. "You'll be coming up on the bridge that connects Orr's Island to Bailey Island, and by the way, most people call it Bailey's Island but it's not. It's Bailey Island."

"I'll make a mental note of that," he said.

"Good, there's going to be a test later. Now this bridge," she began, as they approached it, "is called The Bailey Island Bridge and—"

"I think I can remember that," he said.

"Shush," she said, waving her hand at him. "This bridge is the only 'cribstone bridge' in the world. It's designed to allow the high tides in this area to flow through it without causing any damage to the bridge. The water we are crossing over is called Will's Gut. Turn right at the next road and then stop."

"Will's Gut?" He mouthed the words silently and rubbed his belly.

"Turn right at the next road and stop," she repeated.

He did as she told him, as she continued talking. "Bailey Island was originally called Newaggin. I don't know what that means so please don't ask." He shook his head to indicate that he would not ask. "The first settler on the island was a man named William Black who was the son of a freed slave named Black Will, no relation to you." He shook his head again. "Oh, stop," she said and kept talking. "Black Will was from Kittery, Maine. William Black allegedly sold the island to a reverend named Timothy Bailey. Some say the good reverend bribed municipal officials to find a flaw in Will's title to the land and award it to him. At this point, no one really knows for sure."

"Why do they call it Will's Gut?" he asked.

"I don't know," she said.

"That's cool, Jamie, that you know so much about the state you live in."

"I love Maine, especially the coast. My folks used to bring me and my brother Carl here all the time. My dad taught me the history of the islands. Since I started working and going to Bowdoin, I don't get down here very often anymore. I didn't really have anyone I wanted to come here with until now."

"Until now?"

"Yes, you live in Colorado. We have mountains but not like you have there. Don't you just love the mountains?"

"I do, I used to spend a lot of time there growing up. I went camping and hiking a lot, but this place is as beautiful as any I've seen."

"You're just being nice," she said.

"No, I'm not, my pilot flew us up and down the coast once for about an hour when we were coming back from a mission. I was fascinated. I've heard of the rocky coast of Maine all my life and now I'm here, thanks to you."

"Drive down this road a bit," she said. "We'll have lunch at Cooks Lobster House, my treat."

"Your treat? I can't let you pay for lunch, how would that look?"

"I invited you," she said, emphatically. "Besides, I earn my own money. Please, Will, I want to."

He consented, although it made him uncomfortable, but he was not going to argue with her. She was determined that she was going to pay for their meal. Egg Money didn't have any problem letting Patty pay for their dates. But Will wasn't Egg Money, and it seemed strange to him, but this girl could pretty much do whatever she wanted to with him.

She ordered lobster for them both and showed him how to get the meat out of it. "Wrap your hand around the tail and pull it back, it will separate from the body."

He watched her do hers and then attempted to do the same, but he pulled on it too hard and slung it off the table and onto the floor. She squealed with delight and laughed as he got up, retrieved it, brought it back, and tried again.

"Turn it on its side and push down, to crack it open," she said, demonstrating the technique. Finally, he managed to do as she had shown him and soon he had the meat from the tail and the two claws. "Dip it in the butter," she told him.

"This is really good," he said, with his mouth full.

"You obviously have never had lobster before."

"I've seen pictures of them but I never imagined something so ugly could taste so good."

They ate and talked for about an hour. "It goes good with beer," she said, "but I can only have a beer at home. We're not old enough to drink."

"I like beer but I'm not really a big drinker," he said. "Some of the guys in the squadron—that's all they live for."

They finished eating and Jamie paid the tab.

"Where to now," he asked, as they got in his car.

"Drive on down to Land's End and we'll sit on the rocks of the rocky coast of Maine."

He parked the car at the end of the road. They got out, walked over to the rocks, and found a comfortable spot to sit down. The waves washed against the rocks, occasionally spraying them with drops of seawater.

"This is Casco Bay," she said. "We went on a boat tour out of Portland when I was a little girl. This is my favorite place in all the world. What is your favorite place, Will?"

"Anywhere you are, Jamie," he said.

She looked at him for a moment. "But you don't even know me."

"I want to know you," he said.

They sat in silence for several minutes, until she finally spoke. "Tell me about Colorado."

"I wasn't too forward, was I?"

"No," she said, matter-of-factly.

"There's a place up in Coal Creek Canyon where I was hiking one winter with my dog, Boxer. A little waterfall was frozen solid and I walked out on it, while water was rushing under me, but the ice was thick enough to support my weight. Boxer came out on the ice, too, and we stood there for, a half hour or so, just looking up at the mountains and listening to the water rushing under our feet. It was still and quiet and I imagined it was what heaven must be like. Anyway, that following summer we went back to that spot and Boxer ran out to the waterfall and plunged into the water. I was laughing and he was trying to swim out of it. I could read his mind and I knew he was wondering why the water wouldn't support him. He got out, and we went on down into the Arapaho National Forest and spent the night."

"What happened to Boxer?" she asked.

"Boxer died, he just got old and died."

"I'm sorry," she said.

"That's the problem with dogs, and cats too, if you happen to be a cat person. They don't live as long as people do. So, when you get a dog, or a cat, you know you're in for pain when they die."

"It must have been very hard to leave your home and come so far away."

"I had to move on, it was time. I always wanted to fly, and I wanted to fly in the navy. I didn't want to go to college and become an officer, but I wanted to do pretty much what I'm doing now."

"How long will you stay at Brunswick?"

"Until I get out of the navy, at least that's what they tell me. My obligation is up in '64. I might make a career out of it but I haven't decided yet."

The wind was picking up and the temperature was dropping a bit. She'd had the foresight to tell him to bring a jacket because April in Maine often brought lower temperatures later in the day, especially on the coast.

She huddled closer to him and he put his arm around her. "I have to tell you something," he said.

"You're not married, are you?"

"No," he exclaimed, "of course not. Why would you ask me that? Oh, the guy your dad told me about. No, Jamie, I wouldn't do that, not to you, *or* my wife, if I had one."

"Okay, calm down. I'm sorry I asked," she said. "What is it you have to tell me?"

"We're going on deployment in June."

"But we just met, and you're leaving?"

"I know. They should have warned me not to meet any beautiful girls two months before a deployment. We'll be gone five months. What I want to ask you is if I

can write to you and can I continue seeing you when I
come back."

"Are you sure you want to keep seeing me when you
come back?"

"I'm sure," he said.

"I hope so. I was so disappointed when Sam kept
coming into the shop and you were not with him. I wasn't
about to ask him where you were but I wanted to."

"That's funny," he said, "I couldn't stop thinking
about you but I'd almost given up on seeing you again. I
was afraid that if I went into the cleaners, it would be too
obvious and might spook you. But fate played its hand
and you just happen to be in Clare's Grill that Saturday."
He knew it was more than fickle fate at play in their
meeting, but he wasn't going to tell her that, at least not
now.

"So, you are a fatalist, like I said."

"I guess so, I didn't know I was, but I guess I am."

"When will you leave and where are you going?" she
asked.

"We're leaving June fourth, two days after my birth-
day. It's a split deployment between Argentia, New-
foundland, and Keflavik, Iceland. My crew is going to
Iceland."

"That sounds awfully lonely, Will Cain," she said.
"You'd better write me."

"I will, Jamie Dunham, every day."

"No, you won't," she said.

"I'll try to write you every day."

She had snuggled up against him as they talked and he realized their noses were almost touching. He was almost struck dumb by her face, so much so that he could hardly think straight. He thought she was the prettiest girl he'd ever seen. He cupped his left hand around her neck, pulled her closer, and kissed her. The world around them went away as they sat with their heads tilted together against each other's.

"This is my favorite place too, Jamie."

ᏋᎦᏋᎦ

"Hey, baby, wake up. You were somewhere else. Are you okay?"

"Oh, yeah, I'm sorry," Jamie said. "I was thinking about the first time we came here. I knew I loved you that very first date."

I did, too," he said.

"You knew I loved you?"

"No, that's not what I meant. I knew that I loved you. I didn't know what you thought of me, I was just hoping."

"It was a wonderful time but so scary. When you flew off to Cuba in '62 I cried every day."

"I did, too," he said.

"Oh, you liar," she said, slapping him on his arm. "It was fun for you."

"It was an experience."

"One I hope our kids and grandkids never have to have," she said.

"Yeah, me, too. We'd better get going. Let's bring the whole family down to Cooks tomorrow and then down here. Clare is a born romantic. She's old enough now to appreciate seeing the place where we fell in love."

"I think that's a good idea," Jamie said, and she kissed him.

Richard Dunham's cabin in the woods was a small one-room hunting camp, not too far from Brunswick up, I-295, near Bowdoinham where the Androscoggin and Kennebec rivers mix together.

The cabin was stoutly built and had an oil burning stove but no electricity. There were bunks along the sides of the cabin, enough for four men to sleep. A table in the middle of the room was used as much for playing cards, as it had been for eating, Richard explained. He lit the stove and, as the cabin began to warm up, he motioned to James. "Pull up a chair. Let's chew the fat a while."

James did as his grandfather said and made himself comfortable. Bill started a coffee pot brewing on the stove and then sat down at the table across from James.

"I guess the passion for some things skips a generation," James said, "because Dad has no interest in hunting, but with me, it's all I really want to do. Well, hunting and fishing too, that is."

"And you're working for the forest service now, right?"

"Yes, sir," James said. "It's a dream job. I did inherent my father's love for the mountains, and I go to work in the mountains every day."

"Ah, I wish you could have met your father back when I did, he was such a good kid."

James laughed. "That would have been quite a feat, wouldn't it, Grandpa?"

"Oh, yeah," Richard said, laughing, too. "That's not exactly what I meant to say."

"I know what you meant," James said.

"Anyway," Richard continued, "Jamie told us she was bringing this boy home to meet us. Now I had already seen Will once. Your mother and I used to have lunch at Clare's Grill every Saturday, and incidentally, they named your sister after that café because that's where they say they met. Although she told me later that they had first seen each other at the cleaners where she worked, but anyway, I'm rambling. Did you know about the café thing?"

"I've heard the story, Grandpa."

"Oh, okay, good, I'd hate to reveal a family secret. I thought it was kind of cute but June thought it was silly. So, this young man shows up at my door one evening and he's nervous, I can tell. He was so passionate about his flying in the navy. At that time, he was planning on making a career of it but your mother changed his mind about all that."

James snorted. "Clare still laughs about being named after a café. She really doesn't mind. Most of the friends she's had over the years think it's pretty cool."

"I knew right away they were right for each other. It was just something that felt right. It was the way they looked at each other, the respect he showed her, even when she was throwing a tantrum, which she did quite often."

"She still does," James said, chuckling. "But no one can argue that they were made for each other. Clare is trying to emulate their relationship with a man named Evan Garner, who is working oversees now. Evan is a great guy, he's my best friend, which annoys my sister to no end. But he's one of these individuals, who just can't seem to say, 'I love you.' Clare grew up in a family household where there was never a lack of love. Our mom and dad were always saying it, to us and to each other, but Evan never says it to Clare. He treats her like she's made of gold but he just doesn't tell her he loves her."

"That is strange indeed," Richard said. "Are they planning to get married?"

"I assume so. Evan is a petroleum engineer, working in Indonesia. He told her he's saving money to build them a house in the mountains, when he gets back home, kind of like the house my dad built. But he's never actually asked her yet."

"I just hope she doesn't get hurt."

"I think Clare will be all right," James said. "Though, I worry about her too. She works for the City of Denver and—well, as you know, my sister is a very pretty girl. A guy in her office building made some dirty remarks to her. She told me and Dad about it and it sounded like she handled it okay, but Dad made her promise to report it if it ever happens again. I wanted to go kick the guy's ass but she asked me not to."

"I bet you could do it too, Grandson." Richard said, chuckling. "We couldn't be prouder of you and your sister. We are proud grandparents. Our son Carl married a woman with three children from a previous marriage but they are older than you and Clare so they never came around us much. You are our only grandchildren."

"I'm sorry we don't get to see you more than we do, Grandpa. It's just so far and it's hard to get away from the job."

"I understand, James. You know, your father came to me and said he would stay here in Maine, if we wanted him to. But he had the opportunity to go to work for his father and if I thought it was the best for him and your mother, then he would take her off to Colorado with him."

"I've heard that story too, Grandpa." James said.

"Yes, I expect you have. It was the best for all of

you, and I'm glad he made that choice, even though he took my daughter away from me. He's made her happy and that's all that matters to me."

"I love my parents. They are great people. My mother is so beautiful, Clare was always afraid to bring a boy home to meet them because they kept falling in love with our mother. This guy Evan was the first one who didn't turn goofy when he saw her."

"Well, now I had never heard that story but I'm not surprised. Jamie was always a beautiful girl. And you have her name."

"Yeah, that got me into some fights when I was in school."

"Really, how's that?"

"Some kid would find out I was named after my mother and have something to say about it, I'd dot his eye for him, and tell him if he still thought it was funny, I'd have my mother come to school and dot the other one."

Richard got a laugh out of that.

They sat up half the night talking and laughing, and drank a few beers, but not to excess. James was up at dawn, as was his custom, but Richard was still asleep. So, James slipped quietly out the door of the cabin and slogged off into the snow to inspect his surroundings.

It was quiet, deathly quiet. The sound of his steps, crunching into the snow, seemed to reverberate for miles. He imagined how hard it would be to sneak up on someone without their knowing you were coming. The country was beautiful, just as his mother had described it to him when he was a little boy. She'd told him stories of camping with her father and brother when she was growing up. The beauty of the foliage in the fall, he had seen a couple of times when he was smaller, but he didn't remember much about it. The family had returned a few times when he and his sister were children because the "other" grandparents wanted to see them. But after they grew up, the visits came less and less often. Dad was so busy with the business that he rarely had time for anything else. This was the first time James had been back when he was old enough to go alone with his maternal grandfather, drink beer, shoot guns, and just talk. He believed that, if his parents had stayed in Maine, and raised him here, he would not be much different from the person he was today. And that was taking nothing away from Colorado for, God knows, he did love Colorado.

The serenity and the stillness of the surroundings captured his imagination, and he almost lost himself in it. He stopped walking and closed his eyes, there was no sound, no sounds at all. Eventually the sun would come up and start melting the snow in some places. Water would start dripping and then running into streams. Critters would emerge from their hiding places and start moving around, and the woods would come alive with the sounds of life. But right now, it was silent. He kept his eyes closed for a few minutes until he heard a faint noise in the distance. It sounded like footsteps.

The footsteps were drawing closer. He could not yet tell how close they were to him because the sound carried so far in the morning silence. He continued to keep his eyes closed until the sound of the footsteps stopped. The sound was behind him so he opened his eyes and turned slowly in the direction from which he perceived the sound was coming.

He almost could not believe his eyes. His first emotion was amazement that he was not afraid. He was staring directly into the face of what he first thought was a large dog not more than fifty feet away. It was standing there looking at him, showing no signs of aggression, just looking at him. The pointed ears, with black fur tips and puffs of white fur inside them, the gray and white face and black nose, and general demeanor, quickly told James that this was no dog. He was in a face-to-face standoff with a timber wolf and he had left the cabin without his rifle.

He knew he couldn't run and he knew his chances in a fight were zero to none. So, he stared back at the magnificent creature—not menacingly, it was no time to try his bad-ass routine. He was certain that would not impress his adversary. He didn't dare look away, that would show fear, and he didn't dare make a move. If the wolf attacked, James had no idea what he would do. He would have to figure that out when and if it happened. He struggled to control his breathing and to remain calm so as not to show any fear. Fortunately, he didn't see or hear any accomplices the wolf might have in the immediate area.

James thought for a moment about turning and walking off slowly, but he was afraid the wolf would charge him if he did that, so he continued to stare at the animal. Finally, after what seemed to be an eternity, the wolf yawned widely, and James felt the immediate reflex urge to yawn too. He tried to stifle the urge but couldn't.

Then suddenly the wolf simply turned around and ran off the way it had come. James waited until the sound of the wolf's footsteps could no longer be heard, then he turned and went back to the cabin. He told his grandfather what had happened.

"There are many who say there are no wolves left in Maine but there is an organization, I think in Bangor, that has been documenting sightings that are reported from time to time. We'll call them when we get back home and give them the location here," Richard said. "I wish you'd had a camera so you could have gotten a picture."

"Grandpa, I didn't make a move for the whole time I was looking at that guy. He didn't look like the type that would have let me take his picture."

Richard laughed. "You're right, I'm sorry. I'm just thankful you're okay, James. Take a gun with you the next time you go on a field trip."

"I will, Grandpa," James said.

"I think it would be best if we don't tell your mother about the encounter with the wolf, James, if you know what I mean. I'll get in touch with that organization and report it and if they want to talk to you about it I'll tell them how to reach you."

"I think that's a good idea, Grandpa. She worries too much anyway. She acts like I work in the Wild West now, as it is."

James loved that his grandfather would keep a secret with him from his mother. It was like a bond between them. Men just understood some things that women never could. To a mother, her son would always be a little boy, and she thought of his job like he was going out to play in the woods. James didn't believe that would ever change. He wasn't entirely sure he would want it to change. His dad worried about Clare, and his mother worried about him. It was just the way things were. He guessed he would be the same way when he had kids.

The next day, Will took them all down to Bailey Island, to Cooks Lobster House, for lunch. And then they went down to Land's End to show Clare and James the place they had heard about all their lives, the place where their parents had fallen in love.

"So, what do you think, Clare?" Jamie asked her daughter.

"Oh, Mother, it's just beautiful, so romantic. How could someone not fall in love here? With the waves washing up on the rocks and the sea gulls screeching, or whatever it is they do. I love it here."

"And how about you, son, what do you think?"

James shrugged his shoulders. "I've fallen in love in worst places, I guess."

"Oh, you cad, always got to be the macho man," she said, laughing at him.

"No, Mom, Clare is right, it's really cool. It's a beautiful place. I'm happy for you both."

"Well, thank you. So, you do have a bit of the romantic in you too."

They spent the final night in the Dunham house, had breakfast the next morning, and then drove to the airport in Portland. Soon they were setting down at Stapleton and in their car, heading back up the canyon to the house. It was good to be home, Will thought. He was getting to the point that he didn't much care for being away from his house in Coal Creek Canyon.

He enjoyed the infrequent trips back to Maine but it was always better, the coming home. He went out on the back patio with a cup of coffee and sat there looking up at the mountains.

# CHAPTER 7

*Indonesia*

*October 1986, Jakarta, Indonesia*:

Evan went to work for AOE in the summer of 1986. He spent two months at the company's facility in Houston for training, orientation, and psychological training. He would be contracting for a two-year stint to work in Indonesia. There would be no non-emergency return to the United States for the entire two-year work program. He went back home after training for a week in October to see his family. He spent the week with Clare and once again re-issued his plea that she would wait for him until he got back with enough money to build them a home in the mountains, much like the one she grew up in. Then he flew out of her life.

Evan looked out the window of the airplane at the sprawling metropolis of Jakarta, capitol city of Indonesia. It looked to be more modern than he expected. He could see high-rise office buildings, freeways, avenues, and boulevards. The traffic looked like it could easily rival that along Denver's Valley Highway during any weekday rush hour. He was glad he wouldn't have to drive in it.

He would be meeting a man from the company, an Indonesian man, an Indo, who would accompany him to Makassar, a city on the Island of Sulawesi, where the company facility was located, and where he would be working for the next two years.

American Oil and Exploration, Inc., was able to operate in Indonesia in a few restricted areas, due to a partnership with a company called Pertamina. Pertamina was a state-owned oil and natural gas company based in Jakarta. It was created in by a merger between Pertamina, which was established in 1961, and Permina, established in 1957.

The plane sat down on the runway and taxied to the terminal building. When he entered the concourse, Evan saw a man standing in the crowd holding a sign with his name on it. The man appeared to be in his mid-twenties and was a couple of inches shorter than he was. He was wearing a funny looking hat that Evan recognized as having seen on Indonesian people before. He would learn later that it was called a Peci, among other things. It was also called a songkok, or kopiah and was widely worn in Indonesia, Brunei, Malaysia, Singapore, southern Philippines, and in southern Thailand.

The man, who identified himself as Marcus Tondano, called it a Peci so Evan called it that too.

They shook hands and Marcus led him to a taxi outside the terminal which would take them to a hotel for the night.

They would fly out in the morning to Makassar which was on the island of Sulawesi. Marcus took him to the Hotel Horison. They had dinner and Marcus ordered for them.

"Trust me, Mister Garner. The food is very good. If you don't like Indonesian food, I'll have them make you a cheeseburger."

Evan laughed. "I bet they could, Marcus," he said, "and please call me Evan. I'm just an employee like you."

"Very well, Evan, if you insist. How do you like the hotel?"

"This place is unbelievable. I'm going to write my girl tonight before I go to bed and tell her about it. Can I mail a letter here in the morning?"

"I will see to it," he said.

When Evan got back to his room he found some of the hotel letterhead stationary and sat down to write Clare.

*My darling Clare,*

*I am in Jakarta, Indonesia, at the Hotel Horison. No I didn't misspell it, that's how they spell it here. It's a beautiful place, right on the ocean, but I'm not sure which ocean. I had dinner outside, under a bamboo hut kind of structure, in a jungle with live entertainment. There were sailboats on the water just offshore and some guys parasailing out over the ocean.*

*My guide, a man named Marcus, who was sent by the company to accompany me to the job on another is-land, ordered dinner because I didn't know what any-thing was. It's kind of like Chinese food.*

*I had Ayem Pelalah, which is Balinese Chicken, Gado, Gado a salad, and Suto Ayem, Chicken Noodle Soup. I had to write all this stuff down because I couldn't remember any of the names.*

*I miss you already, baby, and I've only been gone a couple of days. But this will be over before we know it and I'll be home to build us that house.*

*Please don't forget me because I won't ever forget you.*

*Love, Evan*


The next morning, they went to the airport and boarded their plane for the flight to Makassar. The dis-tance between Jakarta and Makassar was 1400 Km or 870 miles, roughly two hours and fourteen minutes in the air.

On the trip, Evan learned that Marcus was twenty-four years-old, two years older than he was. He spoke very good, grammatically correct, English and Evan wondered about that. "How is it you speak such perfect English, Marcus?" he asked him.

"My family was Catholic so I am Catholic and I went to a Catholic school when I was younger. The sisters taught me to read and write English. I am Javanese and I also speak Javanese, and some other island languages."

Evan chuckled. "The company taught me some phrases in Javanese but I don't think I would be very good at it. I had enough trouble with Spanish when I was in school. I don't think I could ever get into all your languages here."

"It takes a lot of time, Evan, but that's why they have me and a few other local people around."

"Your name is not Javanese, is it?"

"No, Marcus is my baptismal name. Catholic Indos often take Latin names for their first name. Tondano is my family name. Many Indonesians do not have family names. They may have two first names, but no surname so to speak. And, like in your culture, many married Indonesian women take the last name of their husbands but not all of them do that. Sometimes they keep their own last name and add their husband's name to theirs. Indonesian names can vary greatly because so many different cultures and nationalities make up our people."

"Where are you from originally, Marcus?"

"My family is from north of Makassar, not far from the company facility. My father was a farmer."

"So how did you end up working for AOE?"

"I received an academic scholarship to the University of North Sumatra. That's a long way from home but it was an opportunity for me and for my family so I took it. I am the oldest of my brothers and my father wanted me to take over the running of the farm when he died, so I chose agriculture as my course of study. But my father died when I was in my second year and we lost the farm so I came home to help support my family. Luckily, I was able to get a job with the company. I've been working for AOE now for two years. I stay at the facility during the week and go home on the weekends. I am very fortunate."

"I'm very sorry about your father and about your losing the farm," Evan said.

"Life sometimes sends us in different directions," Marcus replied.

Evan just nodded. He wasn't sure he could have accepted such a harsh fate so philosophically.

When they arrived in Makassar, a company plane was waiting to fly them to Polewali, 118 miles north in West Sulawesi. From there they were transported by truck to Sipakatau and then on east to the Indonesian offices and operations of American Oil and Explorations. Evan had never felt so far from home and so far from Clare. He was beginning to question his decision to do this. He convinced himself that he must stay focused and keep the big picture in mind.

The living quarters were comfortable and the food was good. The company had made every effort to make the employee's tour as easy and as enjoyable as it could possibly be, given the remote location and the circumstances.

Evan learned that he would be going into the remote sector to work for about three months. That was a normal tour for working away from the main facility. The accommodations were not as comfortable but not primitive. They slept in trailers and the beds were comfortable but the showers and bathrooms were in a separate building about fifty feet from the sleeping quarters. A typical crew consisted of three engineers, a geologist, and two Indo helpers. Evan met his crewmembers the night before they shoved off for the trip.

Harold Parker, the facility manager and overall boss of the whole operation, gathered the men together and told each man to introduce himself and tell a little about himself. The first man, a tall lanky individual with reddish blond hair stepped up first. "Hello, guys, I'm Barry Minton and I'm from Iowa. I am married and have two kids, a boy and a girl."

"Bob Bixby, from Houston, and I was married but my wife couldn't put up with my schedule. I did a two-year contract in Saudi Arabia and, when I got home, she was gone. I don't care, though, she wasn't worth a shit anyway."

"Okay, Bobby, thanks for that positive input," Harold said. "Now you, Barstool, oops, sorry I meant Barstow."

"That's okay, Harold, I'm used to it by now. I'm Barstow Jones and I'm from Anaheim, California. They call me Barstool as you can probably figure out by now. I'm the geologist on the crew."

Evan was last and he thought for a minute about what he would say. He wasn't sure if he wanted to tell them about Clare, after what Bob Bixby had said about his wife but in the end, he said, what the hell and he went on and told his story. "I'm Evan Garner, from Greeley, Colorado. I'm not married but I intend to marry my girl as soon as I get back home from this tour. I plan to build us a house in the mountains with the money I save while I'm here."

"All right," several of them said in unison.

"That sounds like a plan," Barry Minton said.

"I hope it works out for you, Evan," Harold said. "Oh, and by the way, the Broncos lost the Super bowl to the Giants, thirty-nine to twenty."

"Crap," Evan said, "thanks, boss."

Harold introduced the two native helpers, as Perkasa Pertiwi and Suparman Wulandari. "Suparman is pronounced Soo-par-mon but we call him Superman because he's as strong as an ox."

They drove to a small town, more like village, actually, and then turned north and went into what seemed to Evan like the end of the world. It was a jungle and almost impassable terrain. Finally, they got to the site, had dinner, and went to bed. It had taken all day to make the trip.

Jones, the geologist, hiked the terrain and made assessments of where he wanted core samples taken. Then Bixby directed the drilling crews on setting up and making the holes. Minton and Evan worked in the lab analyzing the core samples when they were brought in and then making recommendations on where to sink the next wells.

The work quickly became routine and monotonous but Evan didn't mind it. It kept his mind busy and that made the time go faster.

Evan wrote to Clare every week but he had no idea how long it was taking for his letters to get to her. Regardless, he kept writing. About a month after he was in the field, he received her first letter. He took it outside, found a tree, and sat down to read it alone.

*Dear Evan, I received two of your letters, the first one telling me about the hotel and the next one telling me you had arrived at the company base up in the north part of the other island you're on.*

*The hotel sounded nice and I hope we can go there together someday. I miss you too, darling, I wish you had not gone but I will wait for you, I promise.*

*Please take care of yourself. I love you, Clare.*

She sounded like she was really depressed. He felt bad now that he had taken the job but he was still hopeful that she would come to accept it and be happy about it. She hadn't written very much. He hoped she wasn't growing away from him, but he had to put that kind of thinking out of his mind or else he would lose it.

One day melted into another and, suddenly, this detachment was over. Marcus arrived in the van to pick them up. They packed up their gear and made the trip back to home base. The procedure at the main facility was not much different from the detachment, except there was much more lab work. Core samples were being shipped in from all over the West Sulawesi drilling fields and oil patches. It was very busy, often with sixty hour weeks or more.

They would make two three-month detachments in a year and return to the main base for two three-month stays in the same year. By the end of 1987, Evan was half way through his contract, and he had saved sixty thousand dollars of his eighty-K a year salary, having sent twenty thousand dollars to his folks. He had set up his pay arrangement with the company to make direct deposits into his bank account in Denver. He had made it a joint account with Clare but had not told her. Arrangements were made with the bank to notify her if something happened to him before he returned home. He put the bulk of his money in the joint account and a smaller percentage into an account he shared with his parents. He could draw money from that account for his spending money but he had to go to Polewali to get cash.

Another letter arrived from Clare and he opened it up apprehensively. Her mood was a little better.

*Hi, sweetie, we went to my mother's parents for Christmas and had a great time. Your best friend, my brother, went camping in the woods with our grandfather. James went off hiking by himself and ran into a wolf, a timber wolf, he claimed. He didn't have a rifle so he just stared the wolf down. It made the papers, Grandpa told us after we were back home. There aren't supposed to be any wolves in Maine.*

*Remember the project I told you I was working on? Well, they gave me an extension on my time to finish it, six months. By the time, I finish, it will almost be time for you to come home. I miss you so much. Sometimes I sleep with your picture and pretend you are lying beside me in the bed. But the best part of you is not there, if you know what I mean. I'm so naughty sometimes, I'm sorry. I miss you, oh, I said that, didn't I? Please come home to me quickly.*

*I love you, Evan*
*Your Clare*

Evan read Clare's letter and immediately wished

again that he could go home now. But he had to maintain discipline. He had signed a contract and agreed to work for the company here for the two-year period, and he was determined to keep his word. There was just too much negativity that would come from failing to complete an obligation. He asked Marcus if any American had ever left the job before their contract was up.

"I don't think so, my friend," Marcus answered, "at least not since I've been here. There is too much to lose they tell me. They lose the tax break, you have to pay all the back taxes, and you get blacklisted, and that makes it hard to get a job in the future. Why? Are you considering going home early?"

"No, not at all," Evan said. "It's just that my girl keeps hinting at it in her letters."

"Well, everything I just told you could be company bullshit. I haven't heard any of the employees ever say that, so I don't really know what the consequences might be."

"I know the tax consequence is real, that's for certain."

"Yes," Marcus said, "and that would cost a guy a lot of money."

Evan nodded. "I came here with a plan and I intend to complete it."

"I am happy for you, Evan. That girl will wait. Do you have a picture of her?"

"Sure," he said, reaching into his pocket and retrieving a picture of Clare wearing shorts and a halter top.

Marcus looked at the picture for a moment and then looked up at Evan. "I think you better get home right now my friend," he said, and they both laughed loudly.

"Thanks, Marcus," Evan said, and patted him on the back.

It was the end of March and they were coming up on their next scheduled detachment. They would be heading to a location in a mountainous area called Bakaru, just across the Sungai Mamasa River. "Very beautiful country," Marcus told them.

The night before they pulled out he wrote a letter to Clare.

*My darling Clare, I'll be leaving in the morning for my last three-month detachment before I come home. Only six more months and I'll be 'lying in your loving arms again' (that's from a song, baby). I'm told we are going into the mountains and that it is very beautiful country although I doubt that it is as beautiful as the Rockies, but we shall see.*

*I know this has been hard for you. It has been hard for me too but, it will be over soon and we'll be together again and forever. BTW, I showed your picture to my friend Marcus and he told me I should go AWOL right now. I had to take the picture down from the wall above my desk because the guys kept making lewd remarks about you. It was either take it down or beat the hell out of all of them. I took the easy way out. It must be tough on a woman being as beautiful as you are but I'm glad you are. I still can't figure out what you see in me but I stopped trying a long time ago.*

*I got a letter from my mom and she said you have been coming to see them from time to time. I really appreciate that, thank you. I will write you again when we get to the jobsite in a couple of days but it will take longer to get a letter in and out of there so please be patient.*

*Love, Evan*

The trip to Bakaru was more arduous than any they had made until now. There were no paved roads and the terrain was almost all uphill with steep inclines and treacherous drop-offs on either side of the road. It was slow going. The guys took turns relieving Marcus of the driving duties.

They eventually came to the Sangai Mamasa River, a picturesque river that was alternately fast flowing or lazily moving along depending on the terrain. They forded it at a predetermined high spot with a solid rocky bottom.

As the afternoon approached, the sun was shining on the mountains and Evan noted that the sky was almost as beautiful as the skies in Colorado. He became lost in the myriad of colors splashed across the blue background that reminded him of home. But his attention was diverted by the sudden stopping of the van. He looked to see why Marcus had put on the brakes and saw the man looking up ahead in the road. Five men carrying rifles were spread out across the road approaching the van. Marcus threw the gearshift into reverse and started to back up, but the men started running and firing their weapons at the front of the van.

"What's going on?" someone yelled.

"PKI," Marcus shouted, and kept trying to drive away. The men then shot at the windshield but luckily, no one inside the vehicle was hit.

Marcus then stopped and waited for the men to reach the van. "Remain calm, don't try to resist them, just do what they tell you."

"What's PKI?" Evan asked.

"Communists, anti-government rebels," Marcus said.

The five men reached the van and began ordering everyone out, grabbing at them, dragging them out, and slamming them down onto the ground. Bixby refused to get on the ground and one of the men hit him in the head with the butt of his rifle. One of the Indos started over to see about him but the man, who had hit him with his rifle, yelled something at him in their language and the man stopped.

They assembled them all and told them, by speaking to the two helpers and to Marcus, to start walking. They marched them off into the jungle after setting fire to the van. Evan's first thought was that he might not ever see Clare and Colorado again.

They spent the night on the trail without anything to

eat. The men had food in the backpacks but were afraid if they took any of it out the rebels would take it from them. They had not yet searched their gear which seemed lax to Evan. If he'd had a gun, he might be tempted to try an escape. But that was a moot point because none of them had any weapons.

∽∾∽∾

Nelson Harvey called Clare and asked him to come into his office. She left her desk, walked down the hall. and knocked on his door and, when he said, "come on in," she did.

"Have a seat, Clare," he said.

She pulled the chair away from his desk and sat down, taking her notepad and pen in her hand, and looked up at him waiting for any instructions he might have.

"Oh, you won't need to take notes. I just wanted to talk about the project that you just completed. I'd like to get your thoughts on how it went and if you are satisfied with the results."

"Well, I would like to have completed the project in the original allotted time but it just turned out to be bigger than I first thought it would be."

"Are you satisfied with the help you hired, I mean, were they adequate? Would it have helped to put on more information gatherers?"

"Alex and Marty are excellent employees. I hope

they will decide to stay with the city and I hope there will be jobs available for them. I suppose we could have added a couple of more people but of all the folks I interviewed, Alex and Marty were not just the only ones qualified, they were the only ones who really showed any interest in wanting to do the job. I would have had to go through another battery of interviews, not knowing whether I could find anyone qualified and dependable."

"Okay, I'm sure there will be positions for them in some department in the city structure. Don't worry, if they want to stay here, we want them to. But how about you, Clare, what do you want to do?"

"I haven't really thought about it, Mister Harvey. I didn't know if there would be a job for me after the project was finished."

"And yet you threw yourself into it and gave it all you had, not knowing if you were working yourself out of a job or not?"

"I guess I have my father's work ethic. He taught me a lot about business and responsibility."

"I see," Harvey said and smiled. "Well, that's why we want to keep you here. There are several departments that have expressed an interest in you."

"Really?" she said.

"Yes, really, do you find that hard to believe?"

"I'm flattered but a little surprised, very appreciative though."

"I'll get you a list with the names of the heads of

each department. Let me know which ones you might be interested in and I'll set up a meeting with them for you."

"Thank you, Mister Harvey, "I really appreciate your help."

"You're quite welcome, Clare, and for heaven's sake call me Nelson."

"Will do, boss, thank you again."

ℰⅅℰⅅ

The next morning the men ate the rations they had in their backpacks before their captors had a chance to confiscate any of their belongings. Soon, however, they had them up and walking again. They continued most of the day until they came to a camp in a clearing in the jungle. They were ushered into a fenced in compound. The fencing was chain-link about eight feet high with barbed wire around the top perimeter.

"What the hell is going on, Marcus?" Barry Minton asked.

"I'm not sure, Barry, but I'll try to find out," Marcus answered.

Marcus walked over to the fence and whistled to get the guard's attention. The man came over to the fence and talked for a while to Marcus and then called another man over. That man then left to go to another part of the camp.

"He sent the other fellow to talk to their leader to see if they'll tell us why they took us hostage."

"Who are these people?" Evan asked.

"I think they are elements of the PKI which means Partai Komunis Indonesia, or in English, The Communist Party of Indonesia. It was started by some dissident regional army commanders who opposed the Sukarno government. This was in 1956. They were defeated in 1961 but rogue groups of them still operate all over Indonesia. Nobody has ever reported any of them anywhere in Sulawesi. These guys could just be bandits, but they are dressed like ex-soldiers."

About two hours later, a third man approached the fenced compound and motioned for Marcus to come over. He opened the gate and told him to come with him. The two of them left and walked off into the camp.

"Now they've taken Marcus," Bixby said. "You think he's in on this?"

"I don't think he is," Evan said.

"But how do you know?" Jones asked.

"I don't, but I just don't think Marcus is part of this. It's just a feeling."

A short time later, Marcus returned and was let back into the hostage compound. "They're former PKI, just as I suspected, but now they're just hoodlums and they've taken you hostage. The three of us, he pointed at himself and the two Indo helpers, are collateral damage so to speak. They plan to hold you guys for ransom."

"The US government won't negotiate with terror-ists," Bixby said.

"They'll hit up the company first," Marcus informed him, "if that doesn't work, then they'll try the Indonesian government but I wouldn't count on them doing much. The Americans are your best chance to get out of here quickly."

"Aw crap, this is all I need, I'm scheduled out in six months and this shit happens. Do you know the way out of here, Marcus, I mean if we bust out, can you get us back to home base?"

Before Marcus could answer, Bixby spoke, "I admire your enthusiasm, Garner, old pal, but these assholes will shoot us in a heartbeat. You'd best give up that idea."

"He's right, Evan," Marcus said. "If escape is possi-ble, it might come if they move us, and that will only happen if they know the army is getting close to finding them. The company has undoubtedly alerted the authori-ties by now. It's best to just wait and see what happens for the time being."

The captors started bringing food and that made the men a little more comfortable. Marcus explained that they didn't want the men weak and unable to move fast if they had to pick up and relocate very quickly. That was why they were feeding them regularly.

Two months passed and they still had heard no word as to their fate. The men could only speculate about nego-tiations and how much their captors were asking for or what the company was offering, if anything. Was the government involved? They didn't know, and nobody in the camp was talking to them.

It was June as best they could tell. At least they were still getting paid, the men reasoned. Evan could only imagine what Clare was going through, not receiving his letters and not knowing what had happened. He wondered what the company was telling the families of the men who were missing.

☙❧❧

Meanwhile, back in the world, Clare had interviewed at several other departments in the city and decided to take a position with the Denver Police. She was no longer reporting to the city and county building but rather was working at the Police Administration Building on Thirteenth Street. The job came with her own office and a two thousand dollar a year raise so she was happy about that. The chief asked her to take on the job of monitoring the relationship between the police and the minority population in Denver.

Her family had advised her against taking the job because they thought it might be dangerous. "There are some really bad cops in the DPD," her brother told her. "They are not going to take kindly to a pretty little blonde-haired girl telling them they shouldn't use racial slurs."

"I think I can handle it," she said.

"Baby sister, you don't have a clue what you're getting into," he countered.

"I'm not your baby sister, James, I'm older than you are. I've handled sexual harassment before."

"He's right, though, honey," Will said, "This could be a mistake. You might want to think this over."

But Clare was adamant that she wanted the job. Now, two months later, she still did not regret it. There had only been a few minor complaints. She had seen a training film, made in 1979, in which a sergeant was using terrible racial slurs to some police recruits. She was assured by the current administration that sort of thing no longer was tolerated.

One officer had asked her out but, when she told him she was in a relationship, he was gracious and simply said, "Well, he's a lucky man."

At this point, however, she wasn't sure about the relationship, if it still existed or not. She didn't know where Evan was or what had happened to him. It was driving her crazy but she had to keep on doing her job as if everything was okay in her life. She wanted to just withdraw from life altogether but she knew she could not do that. So, she put on her game face every morning and soldiered on."

Around the middle of June, Clare received a call from George Garner telling her that he had gotten a call from Evan's company. "Evan's crew has been taken hostage by a group of men who were either anti-government insurgents or just plain bandits," he told her.

"Oh, my god," Clare said. "What are they doing about it?"

"They are attempting to negotiate with Evan's captors," was all George knew at that time.

Clare called her mother and told her the news. "Evan's company assured Mister Garner that they would do everything possible to get the men released, no matter how much it cost."

"Well, at least you know Evan is still alive," her mother said.

"It's terrible, Mother," Clare agreed, "but it's better than not knowing anything."

ероко

Another two months passed with no word from the captors on any settlement or agreement about their release. The four Americans were growing more and more frustrated with each passing day.

"We've been with these assholes five months," Bixby said. "I'm thinking maybe Evan is right, that maybe we should try to bust out of this shithole."

"I've been observing their routine for a while," Evan said. "Every so often, the head guy takes the gang out of camp and they're gone for several hours. I don't know where they go, or what they do, but they only leave three men here to guard us. There might be an opportunity there."

"I tend to agree," Barry Minton said. "We have to do something or we may never get out of here. What do you think, Marcus?"

"We'd have to come up with a way to get them to open the gate and come into the compound, then jump the one guy and grab his rifle and shoot the three of them. Are you willing to kill three men?"

"I am," Bixby said. "I'd kill every damned one of them if it means getting out of here."

"Me too," Evan said, "I've spent about as much time here as I can afford to."

"There's a problem for us, the three of us," Marcus said, pointing to the two Indos and himself. "If we do this, we run the risk of getting our families killed. These people will be able to find out who we are and where we live, and they will retaliate. You'll have to lock us in the compound after you get away."

"Damn, I hadn't thought about that, Marcus," Evan said. "I certainly don't intend to put your families in any danger. Do you think they will buy that, locking you guys in the compound? Maybe we should reconsider."

"I don't know, maybe. It's a chance we can take. I'll tell them which way you went, but I really won't."

"You've been a good friend, Marcus, we're lucky to have you with us."

"Thanks, Evan, I just hope you all get back to your

homes. I can understand what it must be like for you being unable to leave here and go home. Here's what we'll do, I'll have Perkasa lay down and play dead, and I'll call the guard and tell him the man is dead so he'll come and open the gate so we can drag him out of the compound. Then Suparman will start dragging him out but will jump the first guard and take his rifle and throw it to Bixby or whoever is closest to him. He doesn't want to shoot a man. Then the American will kill the guards. They do not keep their rifles on safety."

It was two weeks later when the rebel chief led his men out of camp on one of his foraging excursions, or whatever it was they did when they were gone. The men watched them go and looked at each other knowingly.

"It's now or never, guys." Bixby said.

Marcus immediately told the helper, Perkasa, to lie down on the ground and act like he was dead. The man did as he was instructed. Marcus began yelling at the guards in their language and, in a short time, they started walking toward the compound.

The men were breathing heavily now from frayed nerves. Evan had practiced the scenario a hundred times in his mind but the adage, "no battle plan ever survives contact with the enemy," kept popping into his head. He was afraid something would go wrong.

Marcus continued telling the guards that the man on the ground was dead. At first, they were suspicious but Perkasa remained motionless and, eventually, they opened the gate. One guard came in. Superman came over as if he were going to drag the dead man out of the compound but, instead, he grabbed the guard and tossed him against the fence while Evan took the rifle from him and butt stoked him in the face. Blood shot out from his nose and mouth.

The other two guards instantly leveled their rifles at the men in the compound and raked them with automatic weapons fire, killing Bixby, Minton, Jones, and Perkasa. They then took aim at Evan. Marcus yelled, "Watch out!" and jumped in between Evan and the two shooters. Marcus and Superman were hit by multiple rounds from the two guards' rifles, and they fell in a pile on the ground.

Evan fired at the two guards and killed them both. He then realized that the other guard was still alive and would be able to tell the chief that Marcus and the other two Indos had helped the Americans with their escape plan. They would surely seek revenge on the three men's families. He owed it to them to kill the man. He didn't relish the thought of killing a man in cold blood so he didn't think about it, he just did it. He emptied the rifle into the man still lying on the ground.

He then grabbed his backpack and ran out of the camp and into the jungle.

When the bandit leader returned to camp, he flew into a rage. Then, after counting the bodies, he realized that one American had gotten away.

His rage, however, was turned into terror as a contingent of the Indonesian Army suddenly came charging into the camp, with their guns blazing, and tossing grenades. They went through the camp in less than a minute and killed everyone they came across, including the leader of the crew. When they investigated, the hostage compound they identified the American bodies by the only means they had at their disposal, their backpacks. It would be several days before they could get the bodies back to a facility where they could be properly identified. The commander of the force, however, radioed his headquarters and gave the names of the dead Americans: Barry Minton, Barstow Jones, and Evan Garner. One American was missing, most likely lying somewhere in the jungle, dead.

The army notified American Oil and Exploration, which in turn informed the families of the men.

Evan figured he'd run at least a mile before he had to stop and catch his breath. He didn't have a clue where he was, but he knew that, if he could get back to the river they had crossed, then he could at least get to a village or to the ocean. He imagined that there were people following him. He reached for his backpack to get his compass and found that everything had been taken from them. When he opened the backpack, he also realized it was not his backpack. It was Bob Bixby's. In the confusion, he had grabbed the wrong backpack.

He didn't know that his captors had been destroyed and that, had he waited just a little longer, they would all have been rescued. At this point his knowing would have made little difference to him. All he had on his mind now was how to get out of this jungle and back to civilization.

෨෨෨

It was August, two months before Evan was supposed to be coming home. Clare was sitting at her office desk when she heard a knock on her door. "Come on in," she said. It was a very informal work situation.

She was surprised to see her mother and father walk through the door. She sat there a moment staring at them. "What's wrong, Daddy?" she asked.

They continued looking at her, as if the burden of the news they carried was too much to convey.

Clare started crying, sobbing. "Tell me what's happened, something's happened, what is it?"

They came over to her and she stood up and went into their arms.

"Honey," her mother said, "we just talked to Evan's parents. They received word from Evan's company that negotiations had broken down with the rebels. They were being aggressively pursued by the Indonesian Army. They think the men might have attempted to escape, they don't know for sure, but the men were killed, Clare. I'm so sorry, darling."

Clare collapsed into her father's arms, weeping uncontrollably. Her boss, the police chief, came into her office. "Mister and Misses Cain, why don't you take Clare home? Tell her to take as much time off as she needs. Call me when she's ready. There is no pressure on her to come back to work before she's ready."

Will thanked the chief and he and Jamie took their daughter to their car. Jamie sat in the back seat with Clare while Will drove them home. They put Clare in her bed and turned out the lights in her room so she could sleep a while.

"What a terrible thing for the Garners this must be, losing their only son." Jamie said. "I feel so bad for them, and poor Clare, she is so in love with that boy."

A week later Clare called her boss and said she would be back to work the coming Monday morning.

"That's not necessary, Clare, you have plenty of sick days that you have never taken. You don't have to come back to work now if you don't feel up to it."

"No, I want to come back in, Chief. I think I'll handle it better at work than sitting around the house feeling sorry for myself. I need to come back to work."

"Okay, dear, if that's what you think is best. But if you get to feeling bad then take some time off. I'm here for you if there is anything I can do."

"I appreciate everything you've done. I just think I need to get back to work."

Jamie and Will had gone to the police building to re-trieve her car from the parking garage while she was recovering. So, on Monday Clare drove downtown and went back to work.

She had a couple of interviews with one officer who had been accused of mistreating a minority shoplifter he'd arrested, and another with a female officer who was accusing a male officer of sexual harassment.

This was indeed a profession with job security. As long as she would be dealing with human failings there would never be a lack of something to do for a living.

She met first with Officer Johnny McElroy who had been accused of abuse by a citizen he had arrested with items from a department store on his person. The man claimed that McElroy had knocked him to the ground before he arrested him.

"Tell me what happened, Officer," Clare said, after McElroy had sat down across from her.

"Well, ma'am, I was working in the mall and this store called me about a shoplifter that had stuffed a bunch of goods down in his pants and had hauled ass down the mall. So, I head toward the store and I see the guy running toward me and I stop him."

"How did you stop him?"

"I ran into him."

"You just ran right into him?"

"Yes, ma'am, I body blocked him."

"And that seemed the best way to stop a running suspect?"

"It did. He was running pretty fast and there were a

lot of people in the mall. I didn't think he would stop if I asked him to. I didn't know if he was armed or not so I thought the best way to stop him was to knock him down.

"What did you do then, Officer?"

"I cuffed him and checked him for weapons and called the paramedics to take care of the bruises on his face."

"He got the bruises when he went down?"

"That's correct. The paramedics took him to the emergency room and I went with him. When they had doctored his bruises, I took him to Central booking for lock-up."

"The guy claims you hit him."

"I did."

"You punched him?"

"No, I body blocked him, like I said. He was running."

"Oh, okay, aren't there some witnesses?"

"Yes, ma'am, three witnesses, I have their names and phone numbers." He handed the list to Clare.

"Okay, Officer McElroy, I think I have all I need. If the witnesses' stories check out, I don't see any problems. I'll let you know. Be sure and leave me your number."

"Thank you, Miss Cain," he said.

"No problem, Officer. Don't worry, everything will be okay."

As soon as Paige Blankenship walked into her office,

Clare saw the potential problem with putting women in police cars with men. Paige was drop-dead gorgeous. Movie star good looks, brown hair, big brown eyes, and a body that was designed more for a bikini on a beach than for a police uniform, made her an almost-certain personnel problem for the DPD.

"So, what did he say to you, Paige?" were the first words out of Clare's mouth.

"Aw, fuck, where to begin. The asshole never stops. His favorite name for me is sugar-britches, or sweetmeat. You name it, every derogatory name in the book."

"This is Officer Fred Singletary, right?"

"Right, the asshole. I used to partner with Dave Simmons and he never got out of line for a minute. He's married with kids, has a great wife, super guy."

"What happened to Officer Simmons?" Clare asked.

"He was injured in a car chase, he's still recovering. They put me with Singletary and it's been nothing but hell."

"Paige, I have to ask you this. It's strictly routine so don't think I'm defending Singletary because I'm not. But why did you decide to join the police force?"

"And why are you asking me that?"

"Curiosity, mainly, I guess. I mean, you have to know how attractive you are and, to go into a job that is so dominated by men might be taken by some as asking for trouble."

"Then I could ask you the same question. Don't sit

there and tell me that not one single man here has ever said something crude to you or hit on you or made some idiot noise when you walked by. Have you ever considered why *you* took a job in a field dominated by men?"

Clare was stunned for a moment. "That's a fair question, Paige, and I don't have an answer for you. I don't know why I did it, maybe I secretly wanted to find out if I could handle it."

"Maybe so, Clare. Women do it for all sorts of reasons. I know why I did it. My father was a cop and his father was a cop and all my brothers are cops. It's what we do, it's the family business."

"Wow. Okay, thank you, Paige. I appreciate your honesty and I'm sorry for doubting your motives. Now let's you and me nail this sonofabitch."

"Right on, Clare," Paige said, laughing

They put up their hands across the desk and did a high-five.

# CHAPTER 8

*Moving On*

Clare started going to church regularly with her parents every Sunday. She didn't pretend that her going to church would necessarily gain her any brownie points with God. But she hoped that, by her praying, somehow, someway, Evan would be rescued and would come back home to her.

Clare was not the same person she had been up to this time in her life. She seemed to be moving through life without purpose, without conviction, and without the joy of life itself. She used to be able to go out on the patio in the morning with her dad, have a cup of hot tea, watch the sun wash over the Front Range, and feel the exuberance of youth and the joy of breathing mountain air. This always made her happy, now it left her wanting. All her life everything just seemed to work out for her. Her mom and dad were always there to pick up the pieces of her broken toys, her broken relationships, and her broken wings on the rare occasions when she failed to fly. Sometimes her brother filled in for them and when Evan came along, he became her protector. But nobody could heal this hurt, fill this void, or pick up the pieces of her broken life. She would have to save herself now.

It had been five months since Evan disappeared and two months since they were notified that he had been killed. He would have been home by now and they would be married, and getting on with their lives. Instead, she was again avoiding the stare of Jimmy Baxter sitting on the other side of the church trying to get her attention. He had tried to talk to her on two previous occasions and she brushed him off with a wave of her hand. Still, he was persistent.

"I'm not ready to get back into the social scene, Jimmy," she told him several times. "Just leave me alone."

His father, Randall, was always very nice to her and tried to be sincerely comforting but Jimmy's mother, Betty, was bitchy. Clare got the impression that the woman was angry because she wouldn't start dating her son right away. Betty Baxter was always hovering around her son, appearing to be giving him instructions on how to pursue Clare Cain.

Jimmy had completed his degree at Harvard Law School, a year early, by taking summer classes during his under graduate time. He was considered "quite a catch" for most of the young unattached women in Standley Lake Methodist Church. But Jimmy wasn't interested in anyone but Clare.

The Jimmy Baxter controversy was a frequent topic of conversation around the Cain dinner table.

"Jimmy must really love you, Clare," her mother said one evening. "He could have married almost any girl in the church by now. Heaven knows, many girls would be thrilled to marry a Harvard lawyer."

"I wish he *would* marry one of them, Mother, at least that would make him leave me alone."

"Don't be so sure, baby sister," James said, "I have a theory about Mister Jimmy Baxter."

"Oh, really, do you now? I can't wait to hear this. What is your theory?"

"Two things, I think Jimmy is either really and truly head over heels in love with you, I mean to the point of being stupid in love, *or…*"

"Or what?" Clare prompted him, chuckling at his dramatic presentation.

"Or you represent to him the mountain he can't climb, the Rubicon he can't cross, the one thing in life he cannot have. With all his Harvard education, and his family's money, you are the one thing that none of that can buy, persuade, win, convince, or cause to soften toward him. And for Jimmy Baxter, and men like him, that is all that matters. Clare Cain, this lovely creature that we call daughter and sister and treat like a boy, is an itch that Jimmy Baxter cannot scratch. It will eventually ruin his life. Jimmy Baxter will live a life of torment and sorrow because he cannot own the heart of Clare Cain."

"Oh, my," Clare said, astonished, "that was beautiful, James. It was bullshit, of course, but it was such lovely bullshit."

"I think your brother is right," her mother said, "that boy is obsessed with you.

"You want me to kick his ass?"

"No, James, I don't," Clare said. "Why is kicking somebody's ass always your solution to every problem?

"Expediency."

"My concern is that, if the boy really is that obsessed with Clare, he might turn violent," Will said."

"Oh, then maybe I do need to kick his ass," James said.

"No, son, you don't need to kick his ass. Remember, he's a lawyer, but it won't hurt to let him know you're keeping an eye on him."

"Dad, are you men all the same? You all seem to have this macho gene that makes you have to know if you can piss farther than the next guy."

"That's very important, darling," Will said, "A man has to know where he stands in the distance pissing event."

"You're all twisted," she said, and threw up her hands in mock outrage. They all laughed loudly.

"Laugh all you want gentlemen. If your 'baby sister,' as you like to call me, and your daughter, ever does decide to move on with her life, I'll probably marry a cop. I get at least two proposals a day from the cops I work with. How would you like that?"

"I wouldn't like that," James said.

"If he's a good guy, I'd be okay with it," Will said. "Two proposals a day, Clare, really?"

"That may be a slight exaggeration," she said, "half of them are propositions not proposals."

"Well, that makes me feel a lot better," her father replied.

ↄ◦ↄ

Fred Singletary received a written warning that went into his permanent file, a week off without pay, and reassignment to a different sector in the city. He was also ordered to attend sensitivity training that introduced him to proper procedures involved in working with female police officers.

Paige Blankenship and Clare became friends and often began having coffee together when the opportunity

presented itself. Paige received a new partner and reported to Clare that everything was going fine and that all the
male officers were treating her as an equal.

Clare continued to be asked out by men in the department, but she politely declined, telling them that she
was still recovering from her fiancé's death. She wasn't
sure how long she could continue to carry on with that
excuse. She was slowly coming to grips with the reality
that Evan was not coming back. As painful as it was to
face the truth, she had to accept it.

There was a homicide detective named Allen Petty,
who had been assigned to accompany Clare on several
interviews in neighborhoods the chief was not comfortable sending her into alone. Allen was divorced, not an
atypical marital status for homicide detectives, and was a
generally likeable man. He was considered one of the
best and most trusted cops in the city. This was one of the
reasons why he was given the job of being Clare's protector. They had maintained a professional relationship, although Clare could sense that Allen wanted more from her
than he let on. Eventually, on another assignment, he finally asked her out to dinner.

"I would go, Allen, but I'm just not ready yet. I appreciate your asking me. You're a nice man and this is
not a slight against you. I just haven't started dating anyone yet."

"I have feelings for you, Clare, strong feelings, and
it's not just your looks. It's much more than that. I've re-

ally fallen for you in the time we've been working together. If you'll just give me a chance, I'll prove it to you."

"I'm just not ready yet, Allen," she said, "I'm sorry."

He remained silent the rest of the day and Clare could only speculate about how he took her rebuff. When she got back to her office, she left a message for Paige Blankenship asking her to call back. Paige showed up at her office at the end of the day.

"What's up, girl?" Paige said, as she came into Clare's office.

Clare told her about Allen Petty and his advances toward her.

"I know Allen. Well, it's more like I know *about* Allen, than I know him. He's kind of quiet, seems nice, but he went through a messy divorce a couple of years ago. He caught his wife with another guy and beat them both up. No charges were ever filed because he's a cop and blue protects blue. Did he tell you he's in love with you? He's rumored to have done that with other women."

"He did. Well, he said he'd fallen for me. That's why I called you. I haven't even gone out with the guy and he said he's in love with me. That's just weird."

"He may really be in love with you, Clare, men are weird fuckers, believe me."

"Oh, I know they are. Evan is, or was, a wonderful man but he had some hang-ups that just drove me mad."

"I'm guessing that Allen just wants to screw you.

Hell, Clare, every man in the building wants to screw you and probably some of the women."

Clare's eyebrows went up, "I doubt the chief does," she said.

"No, he does, he's just too decent a man to admit it to anyone."

They both laughed at that.

"So, what should I do?"

"Keep it professional, above all else. If he pushes too hard, you may just have to tell him that you don't feel that way about him and you don't think you ever will. It's the curse of being a beautiful woman, Clare. I've lived with it all my life."

"I know, Paige, that's why I asked for your help. Thank you for coming."

"Keep me informed on this if you will. These things can get out of hand if you're not careful."

"I will, and thanks again," Clare said.

This was not in her job description, Clare was thinking. When the chief laid out all the duties that her job entailed, he failed to mention things like this. "Oh, by the way, sugar-pants, you'll also have to contend with two thousand or so men, every day, who want nothing more, than to get you in bed. Are you okay with that?" he should have told her.

Would she still have taken the job? Probably, but at least she would have been prepared.

And the weekend offered little relief. At church on

Sunday there was Jimmy Baxter. "Can I take you to lunch after church?" he asked her as she walked in.

"I usually go to lunch with my family, Jimmy."

"I know, but I just want to talk. I promise, no funny business."

She wrote it off to a moment of weakness, and that she was under a lot of stress, because of the business at work but, in any case, she agreed to have lunch with Jimmy.

"Where would you like to go, Clare?" Jimmy asked her as they drove away from the church.

"I don't care, wherever you pick."

"Okay, there's a place not too far from here I like. We'll try that if it's okay with you."

"It'll be fine," she said.

"Listen, Clare, I know you've always thought that I'm an oaf—and you're right, I have been most of the time you've known me. But I've changed, I promise you I have. College and law school have matured me. I've grown up, I guess is what I'm trying to say."

"I'm not ready to start dating yet, Jimmy."

"No, I know, and I'm not asking. I just want to clear the air. When we were in high school, every guy in school wanted to go out with you, and I was no different. I just wanted to be the one who did it. When you went to the prom with me, it was like I'd won the lottery. I was the most popular guy in school. You were so beautiful— still are, I mean."

Clare smiled at his rambling, and he continued.

"And when I told you I loved you, that was no bull-shit—oh, I'm sorry, I mean that was the truth. I did love you back then. I think I probably still do."

"I was pretty arrogant sometimes, I suppose. I understand how you feel and I appreciate your sharing this with me now. But I'm just not ready yet to start seeing anyone. It's just too soon."

"I know, and I'm not asking you to start going out with me on a regular basis. I'm just asking you to give me a chance when you do get to that point. At least think about it, will you?"

"Okay, Jimmy, I'll think about it."

"That's all I'm asking," And he seemed content with that for the time being.

Clare decided that perhaps it was time that she move on with the rest of her life. And the first step she needed to take in that was moving out of her parents' house. She decided to get her own apartment in Denver, closer to her job. At some point in time, she might meet a man that she wanted to start seeing on a regular basis, and it would be a little awkward for him to pick her up at her daddy's house way up in Coal Creek Canyon, especially if she decided to have a "sleepover."

Against the wishes of her mom and dad, Clare rented a two-bedroom apartment not too far from UC Denver and close to her work. She chose a two-bedroom in case she might decide to take in a room-mate sometime in the future. It was a nice apartment in an upscale area near downtown. Her dad and brother helped her move all her stuff in and checked out the neighborhood surroundings.

"I'm not really ready for this but I guess I'll have to live with it," Will said.

"Oh, Daddy, I'm a big girl now."

"Girl being the operative word here."

She hugged him. "Woman, I meant to say."

Her first night in the apartment wasn't traumatic but it was a milestone in Clare's life. She had an apartment when she was in college but that was different somehow. This time she was really on her own. No Mommy, no Daddy, no Evan, she was on her own. It was empowering and frightening at the same time. She was on the second floor and the apartment was on the west side of the building. Coffee on her patio in the morning, watching the sun rise on the mountains, was a moving experience, and she determined that would be her daily routine. She would enjoy being so close to her job, not having to brave the elements driving down the canyon every morning and evening and not having to fight Denver traffic. It would give her an extra three hours a day to add to her life. Not too shabby, she decided. She had promised her folks that she would continue to go to church on Sunday and come to the house for lunch afterward, and she did continue that routine.

At night, she was lonely and found herself thinking about Evan—every night, it seemed. She often cried herself to sleep. What would she do now that she knew Evan was dead? It was almost too awful to imagine but she had to accept it. What could she do now? She didn't know, and she didn't have anyone she could talk to about it, or at least she didn't have anyone she wanted to burden with her troubles. Could she go on? she had to, yes. So, she got up every morning, put on her "game-face," and walked into the DPD building like she owned the place, turning men's heads with every step she took.

Jimmy Baxter joined his father's law firm and was now practicing law in Denver. He asked for her phone numbers and she gave him the number at her apartment but told him not to call her at work. She didn't want to take a chance that he might show up at her office. He started calling her at night and, on occasion, she would talk to him but more often she just let the recorder take his message.

It soon became clear that Allen Petty was not going to go away nor was he going to be content to give Clare time to get ready to start dating again. He pursued her more aggressively, to the point that she was about to request another escort for her special interviews in the field. He dropped in to her office more often than he had a need to, wanting to take her to lunch or just to see if she was okay.

Clare was becoming more and more concerned every day. They had an assignment the coming week and she decided she would take that opportunity to clear the air with him and do what Paige told her to do. She would tell him that she was never going to feel the same way about him, as he felt about her. She hated that it had come to that but he gave her no other choice.

They were in a project to interview a woman who had claimed two policemen had verbally abused her, using racial slurs, and had roughed up her son when he came to her defense. Allen sat in the woman's room with Clare, as a witness and, in the event, someone in the apartment tried to harm her. When the interview was concluded, they left and walked down the stairs to the first floor. They found themselves in a foyer all alone with not another person in sight or earshot. Allen started to speak to her.

"Clare," he said, "I have to tell you—"

"Allen, we need to talk about this—" she said, cutting him off.

He immediately reached around her with his right hand and pulled her tightly against him. Then he put his left hand behind her head, pushed her lips onto his, and started kissing her, very passionately and prolonged. He didn't seem inclined to stop. She began struggling to get free from him but he held her even more tightly. She bit his lip and drew blood. The man yelled loudly and removed his mouth from hers.

"You bitch," he yelled at her and slapped her hard across the left side of her face.

"You, asshole," she yelled back at him. "You stupid,

thick-headed asshole. Why couldn't you just take no for an answer? Why couldn't you just leave me alone?"

He slapped her again. She cried out loudly from the pain and staggered back against the wall of the foyer. She managed to regain her balance and kicked him in the crotch, as hard as she could. He screamed and bent over with pain. Clare started to run toward the door. But Allen grabbed her foot and her shoe came off. She pulled her foot loose, then she took off her other shoe, ran to her car, and drove away, leaving Allen there in the building.

She drove back to the police station, went immediately to the chief's office, and explained what had happened. She then had to retell the entire history of her dealings with Allen Petty and how he had expressed his love for her and that she had gently rejected his advances. Paige was brought in to confirm that Clare had told her about Allen and that she, Clare, was in no way encouraging him to continue his interests in her.

Allen lost his job and spent six months in jail for assaulting Clare. Clare had to testify against him in court, as did Paige Blankenship. Jimmy Baxter was starting to look safe to Clare about this time.

One Sunday, a few weeks later, after lunch with Clare, Jimmy Baxter drove out to Red Rocks. He parked in a space facing the rock formations.

"I've always loved this place," he said.

"Me too," Clare replied, "this is Denver's 'Garden of the Gods.'"

"Oh, like in The Springs?"

"Yes," she said," not as majestic but still beautiful."

"Not as beautiful as you, Clare."

She pursed her lips and just looked at him as if to say "Really, that's all you can say?"

"Oh, come on, Clare," Jimmy said. "You have to know by now. I can tell you how many men who have seen you, think you're beautiful, me included. Do you want to know?"

"How can you know that?"

"Do you want to know?" he persisted.

"Sure, go ahead."

"All of them, every one of them," he said, "except maybe the gay wads."

"Now you're being silly, Jimmy."

"I know, but what I'm trying to say is that in high school every guy wanted to date you, whether they really knew you or not. They wanted to date you because of the way you looked. I did too, but I was lucky, I got to know you because you went to my church and I wanted to date you because I knew what kind of person you were—and because you were beautiful and because it would have made me the envy of every guy in the school."

"That was, very superficial," she said.

"I know but it's the truth and I did love you. I still do. I love you, Clare, and if you will marry me, I'll do everything I can to make you happy. I know you're hurting right now and I'm not pressuring you, but just tell me you'll think about it."

Clare lowered her head and spent some time in deep thought. Jimmy waited, for as long as he could, and then touched her shoulder.

"Clare," he said and she looked up but not at him. She stared out the window and it appeared that she was only vaguely aware that he was even in the car with her.

"I will marry you, Jimmy," she said and paused a moment to gauge his reaction. He started to open his mouth and she held up her hand to keep him from talking. "But I can't promise you that I will ever fall in love with you. I will share your bed and be a wife to you, and I will never cheat on you. I will treat you with respect and never ridicule you in front of other people and I ask that you do the same for me."

"Oh, my God, Clare. I wasn't expecting that. Of course, that's fine. Everything you said is fine. Shit, I can't believe this. Thank you, Clare. When can we do it, get married, I mean?"

"Maybe a month from now, if that will work for you."

Jimmy was about to lose his mind. His dreams had just come true and he almost could not contain himself. "Can I kiss you now?"

"No, you're too worked up, wait until you calm down."

After a few minutes of what he considered casual

conversation, Jimmy turned to her again. "Can I kiss you, now, Clare?

"Okay, Jimmy, you can kiss me now," she told him.

He moved over next to her, put his arm around her, and pulled her gently to him. He kissed her, and it was not the boorish kiss she was expecting but rather tender and sweet.

"You've come a long way since high school, Jimmy, that was a very nice kiss."

"Thank you, Clare. I really do love you."

"I believe you," she said, "and I'll be cognizant of that, but like I said before, I can't promise that I will share the same feelings that you have for me now."

"If you will just try, I'll be good to you, I promise. What do you want to do now?"

"I really need to go home. Can you take me back to the church so I can get my car?"

The family was in shock when she told them she was going to marry Jimmy Baxter. They wanted to know why, since she had always expressed such a vehement disgust for the man.

"I wasn't going to tell you this but I have to now, to explain my decision to marry Jimmy." She told them about Allen Petty, how he had assaulted her, the whole story. "It took two weeks for my bruised face to heal. That's why I didn't come home for those two weekends. You remember?"

They nodded.

The chief told me I could take off until I healed up but I wanted those bastards to see what one of them did to me."

"How did the other policemen act toward you, darling?" her mother asked.

"They were the sweetest things. You wouldn't believe how nice they were, telling me how sorry they were for what Allen did. One of them said he wished that he'd been there so he could have stopped him. I got a lot of attention, and candy and flowers. It was really sweet."

"They'll be looking for some payback before too long, baby-sister," James said.

"What do you mean?"

"They'll be trying to get you off your feet again as soon as they think you're back to being Clare the indomitable."

"Oh, James, I might have known you would say something like that."

"What happened to the man who hurt you, Clare?" Will said.

"The man is in jail now but, as long as I am unattached and in the workplace, this business is not going to stop."

"So, you're marrying Jimmy to keep men from hitting on you, dear?" her mother said.

"It's not just that, Mother. Evan is not coming back and I'm never going to fall in love again. I want to have children and I can't do that without a husband—well, I can but I'm not going to. I have to move on, that's pretty much the bottom line."

"Oh, Clare, I hate to see you get into a loveless marriage. You'll meet someone someday, honey, I know you will."

"How, Mother? I'm surrounded by cops and Jimmy Baxter. I'm not going to marry a cop and worry, every time he walks out the door, that he might not come home that night. Jimmy is safe and he comes from a good family."

"But will being married to Jimmy Baxter make you happy, honey?"

"I'm never going to be happy again, Mother."

# CHAPTER 9

*Deliverance*

Evan started running again but then decided, that no one was chasing him. So, he stopped and began a steady walk at a pace he felt he would be able to maintain without having to stop too often. When the sun started going down, he determined which way was west so he knew he was heading toward the river they had crossed. Once he got to the river, he would either follow it on foot or try and craft some sort of raft to float on down to a village or town. He knew the river passed close to the AOE main base so if he could get there then he could get back home.

It started raining and Evan checked the backpack.

The bad guys had taken everything they deemed of value. The compass was gone and the hunting knife, first aid kit, and snake-bite kit. Bixby's ID was in the secret compartment. That was great, he thought, if he died now, and was found dead, they'd send his dead ass to Texas. If the others were ever found, Bixby would be mistaken for him and Evan's parents would be notified that he was dead. Of course, there was the possibility that, should the authorities find them, their bodies might be identified and then they'd be wondering where Evan was. That would probably be a good thing.

He collected some rainwater in a leaf and filled it over and over until he'd had enough. Then he continued his trek westward. He was walking downhill so he figured he was headed in the right direction. He found a clearing and tried to get some sleep. As he drifted off, he thought about Clare. What she must be thinking, wondering where he was, if he was dead or alive. He was angry, angry at the company and at the Indonesian government. All they would have needed was two or three men with automatic weapons to accompany them on their detachments. The five men would not have tried to take them hostage had they known it would mean a gun fight. At least that was his theory.

He awakened at first light and started walking again. He was hungry now and had no idea where he would get food. He found some berries but was afraid to eat them so he picked them and put them in the backpack until such a time that he got so hungry he didn't care if the berries killed him. He kept focused on Clare's face. All he could think about was her face. It was all that kept him going.

*Ah, Clare*, he thought in the deepest recesses of his mind and heart. *My sweet, Clare*. She wasn't just another woman. Clare was life itself to Evan.

e/ɔe/ɔ

Clare picked up her mail, went to her apartment, sat down on the couch, and started looking through her letters. There was an envelope from the Internal Revenue Service.

A letter from the IRS was always scary, even if you hadn't done anything wrong, so she opened it curiously and slowly. It was the strangest letter. It informed her that she owed interest on $4,000.00 she had made on savings in her bank account, an amount of approximately $450.00.

Clare was dumfounded. The bank listed was not even her bank. And no way had she made $4,000.00 in interest. She barely had that much money in her account at any given time. The next day she went to the bank, the IRS had named in the letter they sent her.

"Do you know an Evan Garner, Miss Cain?" the bank manager asked her.

"Yes, he was my fiancé," she said.

"Are you aware that you have a joint savings account with him at this bank?"

"No, sir, I wasn't."

"Yes miss, you do. Mister Garner set up the account before he left for his overseas job. The balance in the account is a hundred and twenty-thousand dollars."

Clare was struck dumb. "Are you serious?"

"I am," the man answered. "Did he not tell you?"

Clare started crying, softly at first then broke into sobs. One of the women in the bank came over, put her arms around her, and held her until she could speak again.

"Evan was killed in Indonesia, and I never knew he had opened an account here and put me on it, too. He was going to build us a home in the mountains when he got back."

The lady, who had come over to comfort her, started crying too and the bank manager just sat there. "I wish you two would stop that," he said, "before I start crying, too."

"I'm sorry," Clare said.

"Was Mister Garner the kind of man who would put this much money into a joint account for you and not tell you about it?" he asked her.

"Yes, yes, that's exactly the kind of man he was."

ຉຉຉ

After two days Evan came to the Sungai Mamasa

River. He had eaten the berries, found and picked some more, and eaten them, too, and had not died yet, but he was still hungry. He walked along the river for about five miles until he spotted a tree that had fallen into the water. It had almost separated from its trunk and was about to float off downstream. The tree had two forks at the top forming a Y.

He hustled down to the water's edge, jumped into the water, and started trying to maneuver the tree out away from the bank. He had a mind to climb up on the tree and rest between the forks that formed the Y. He managed to push the thing out into the stream and get aboard, but as he was putting his backpack in the area between the two forks, and securing himself firmly on the tree, he felt something stick him in his foot that was still in the water.

"Shit, what was that?" he said out loud.

His position on the tree wouldn't let him pull his foot up to look for fear he would roll off the tree. He looked back and saw what looked like some kind of water snake swimming away from him toward the other bank of the river. "Sonofabitch," he cursed at the snake but that did not ease the pain in his foot.

Although his foot burned as if it was being roasted on a spit, Evan felt himself getting dizzy. He was afraid he was going to pass out. He was afraid that, if he passed out, he would roll off the tree and drown, so he struggled to secure himself to the tree a little better. He pulled his body farther up into the forks so that if he did roll either

way he would not roll off. Then he slowly lost con-
sciousness.

About fifty miles downriver, a man was fishing with
his son from a small boat on the water. The young boy
spotted a tree floating by, with a man lying on it. The boy
ran to the front of the boat and tugged on his father's pant
leg.

"Papa, Papa," the boy said, and pointed at the tree.

The man grabbed his pole and quickly started push-
ing his boat into the path of the oncoming makeshift raft.
The tree bumped into the boat and swung around until it
was parallel to it. The man and his son managed to lift the
man off the tree and into the boat. They also picked up
his backpack. Then they then poled over to the bank of
the river, and the man told his son to run and get some
help. The boy hustled off up the side of the riverbank.

In a short while, the lad returned with his two older
sisters. The two girls and their father carried the man to
their house which was not far from the river. They laid
the man down on a couch and tried to make him comfortable. He looked dead but he was breathing. His right foot
was swollen and had turned black. The man's wife made
up a compound, spread it on the foot, and wrapped it in a
cloth tightly. The man left to walk to the nearest village
to get help.

Two days later, the man returned in a police van with
two deputies from the city of Polewali. They transported
the man to a hospital in Polewali and he was put into in-

tensive care. They diagnosed the foot injury as a snake bite and started giving him antibiotics right away, although the swelling had been reduced somewhat, by the compound that had been put on his foot by his rescuer's wife. The man remained unconscious, however.

They examined his backpack, looking for some identification and realized that he was an employee of American Oil and Exploration so they contacted the company facility. A local representative showed up right away, assessed the situation, and decided to contact the main office in Houston.

The CEO of the company, Charles Lincoln Griffin, and Vice President, Henry Morrison, called for the company jet to take them to Indonesia. They would have to fly into Makassar first to refuel and then fly up to Polewali. Griffin believed this was a serious situation that demanded his personal attention.

The next afternoon, he was talking to the doctor who was attending to Evan, who was still unconscious. "Can we move this young man, Doctor?" Griffin asked.

"Where do you want to take him, Mister Griffin?" the doctor asked.

"I'd like to get him to Hawaii where he'll be closer to home when he comes out of this coma he's in. I'm going to have to take him to Houston but I don't want to take a chance on going that far all at one time.

"I don't recommend it but if we send a nurse and some equipment with you, I'll be okay with it."

"Then let's do it. Get him ready and get me a nurse. I'll see that she gets back home. This young man has been through hell, while on the job for our company, and I want to make every effort to reunite him with his family."

"Yes, sir." The doctor snapped his fingers and shouted orders, and people started moving.

They loaded Evan onto the AOE corporate jet. The nurse situated herself in the back next to him, and they took off for Hawaii.

When Evan opened his eyes, he was looking up at fluorescent lights in, what looked to him, like a hospital room, and he had no idea where he was. He lay there about a half hour, as best he could figure, just listening to the sounds and activity going on around him. The last thing he remembered was climbing onto a tree and getting bitten on the foot by a snake. Now he was somewhere and he was either dead or not dead. Whichever it was, it wasn't too uncomfortable. His name was Evan Garner and he was from Greeley, Colorado. He was in love with a girl named Clare. Yep, that was him. He was still alive but he didn't know where he was.

A nurse came into his room and started checking the thing stuck in his arm. She hadn't noticed that he was awake.

"Who are you?" he asked.

"Oh," she yelped. "You scared the hell out of me."

"Sorry."

"That's okay," she said. "When did you wake up?"

"I don't know," he said. "Where am I?"

"You're in Queen's Medical Center in Honolulu, Hawaii."

"Really?"

"Yes, really," she said and giggled. "I'm going to notify your doctor."

"Okay."

The room was soon busy with activity. Henry Morrison, the VP of AOE, was still on scene to handle Evan's case, of which the most interesting part was yet to come.

Morrison came into the room and walked over to Evan's bed.

"How are you feeling?" he asked him.

"Okay, I think," Evan said. "That's just a guess, I'm not a hundred percent sure."

Morrison laughed. "I'm not surprised. We've been trying to contact your family but no one answers any of the phone numbers we have. We've sent people out to your parents' house but we were told they no longer live there. Your ex-wife was uncooperative so we didn't get much help from her."

"I've never been married," Evan said.

"What?" Morrison said, a bit confused at that response.

"I've never been married, I'm getting married when I get home."

"I don't understand, Bob, your employment record says you are divorced."

"My name isn't Bob." Evan said.

"What?"

"My name isn't Bob"

"What is your name, son?" Morrison asked him, now totally confused.

"I'm Evan Garner from Colorado."

"Oh shit, oh holy shit. What the hell have we done?" Morrison exclaimed.

"It's not your fault, sir," Evan said. "When we tried the escape, it went badly and everyone was killed before I got the rifle away from one of the guards and killed him and the other two. The AOE employee Marcus Tondano jumped in front of me and was killed, saving my life. After I killed the guards, I grabbed Bob Bixby's backpack by mistake. I figured that everyone would think I was dead and he was alive, but there was nothing I could do about it. It's not your fault."

"Then we have to let your family know you're okay."

"No, don't call them. I want to surprise them. I need to get to Denver. I have to get to my girl."

"But they think you're dead, Evan. Shouldn't we call them?"

"If you don't mind, Mister Morrison, I just want to go to them first."

"Okay, if that is what you want. As soon as they

check you out and release you, I'll take you to the airport."

"I don't have any ID or any of my credit cards or anything."

"Don't worry, Evan. I'll call ahead and reserve you a rental car, and I can get you a temporary company ID card and a cash advance against your back pay, then we'll get you on your way home. As soon as you're ready to go back to work, get in touch with me, and we'll find a place for you. You will get your back pay as soon as I notify the main office."

"Thank you, Mister Morrison."

"No, thank *you*, Evan."

ℰↄℰↄ

Clare and her father were sitting on the back patio of his home in the canyon, watching the sun go down over the Front Range.

"Well, my darling daughter, two more days and you'll be walking down the aisle on my arm. Since the day, you were born I have always imagined what a happy day this would be. But it just doesn't seem to be shaping up that way. I just wish there was some way I could change things for you."

"Thank you, Daddy, you've always fixed things for me all my life, but grown-up life just doesn't always work out the way you plan it, does it?"

"I guess not, honey, but your mother and I have prayed for you, for your happiness. We have prayed that, no matter what, you will be happy. That's all I have ever wanted for you, that you'll be healthy and happy. Some things are just too big for daddies, that's when you have to let God step in.

"I just don't think I'll ever be happy again, Daddy."

"I won't buy a pound of that. I think you *will* be happy again, Clare."

# CHAPTER 10

*Speak Now*
*Or forever hold your peace*

Evan arrived at Stapleton Airport at eleven am, October twenty-fifth, retrieved his luggage and rental car. He thought about going to his parents but a foreboding, nagging, feeling told him to go to Clare's house first. It was Saturday so traffic was not too bad, and he reached the foot of the canyon in good time. He noticed James's truck in the driveway when he pulled into the property.

When James came to the door, he looked like he'd seen a ghost. "Holy fuck, Evan! Holy fuck!" he yelled.

He repeated it several times.

"What, what, James, what?" Evan shouted.

"They told us you were dead, Evan. Your company and the state department said you were killed. Holy fuck, what are you doing here?"

"It was a mistake, a mix up. I have to call my folks. Can I use your phone?"

"You can but there's something else I should tell you first."

"Okay, what's that—hey, where's Clare?"

"That's what I have to tell you, Evan. Clare is getting married today."

"Married, why? I mean where, when?"

"She's marrying this asshole in our church."

"Who?"

"It doesn't matter who, he's an asshole."

"You mean today, like today, today?"

"Yes, today."

"What time today?"

"About one o'clock, I think."

"Why aren't you there?"

"Because he's an asshole. I can't stand the guy."

"What time is it now?"

"We've got time, get in my truck."

Evan got into James's truck and James burned rubber getting out of the driveway and onto the road. He was rounding the curves on the narrow mountain road at breakneck speed.

"Try not to kill me before I get a chance to let your sister know I'm not dead," Evan said.

"Are you kidding me. I've been driving this road since I was nine."

"Nine?

"Fifteen."

"Does she love this asshole?" Evan asked.

"No, hell no," James responded.

"Then why is she marrying him?"

"We thought you were dead."

Evan just nodded and started telling Jamie how he had escaped.

"That's great, Evan, but listen to me. When we get there, and hopefully we can get there before it's too late. But when we get there you have to tell her you love her."

"But I do love her. I've loved her since the first day I laid eyes on her. I loved her before I knew her name."

"But you never told her that. Women are funny like that, you gotta tell them."

"All right," Evan said. "Then step on it, we have to stop that fucking wedding."

When they reached Eighty-Sixth Parkway, the street the church was on, James was doing eighty miles an hour. A Colorado State Trooper spotted him, turned on his emergency lights, and gave chase.

"What do we do now?" Evan asked, concerned.

"Don't worry, I can get to the church before he gets to us."

"You'd better stop, James."

"I'm not stopping."

"He's a state trooper, you have to stop."

"We have to stop that fucking wedding, remember? Just hang on."

The police car stayed after them and was gaining, but they were getting close to the church. When they got there, the parking lot was full so James stopped the truck at the outer edge of the lot. They both piled out and started running toward the front door. The trooper pulled in right behind James's truck and watched the two men running across the parking lot.

James literally crashed through the front doors of the church with Evan close behind. Then he slowed to let Evan take the lead. Everyone in the place except the bride and groom turned to see what had caused the rude interruption. Jimmy and Clare were facing the pastor but Evan couldn't hear what was going on.

"*Wait*!" he shouted at the top of his lungs. "Wait, stop the wedding, she can't marry him."

Clare and Jimmy then turned to see who this "madman" was. When she saw it was Evan, she put her hands to her face and screamed.

"Evan, Oh my God, Evan! What are you doing here? I thought you were dead." She almost fainted but one of the bridesmaids grabbed her. Clare's mother rushed up, took her hand, and steadied her.

Jimmy turned away with a look of disgust on his face. "Aw shit!" he said.

The pastor looked at him with disapproval. "Really, Jimmy, in the church, at the altar?"

"I'm sorry Pastor," Jimmy said.

"You can't marry him, Clare, you have to marry me," Evan shouted.

"But you never asked me, you never even said you loved me." Clare was crying now. "Why did you never tell me you love me?"

"I know, baby, because I'm an idiot, but I'm telling you now. I love you, Clare. Will you marry me?"

"Yes, yes of course I will, Evan. You know I will." Clare lifted her hands up over her head and exclaimed loudly, "Thank you, God, thank you Jesus."

Jimmy was mad now and he told some of his friends to get James and Evan out of the church. "It's too late," he said. "We've already said our vows."

"No, we didn't," Clare yelled at him through the salty tears in her mouth. "You said yours but I didn't say 'I do' yet. I'm sorry, Jimmy, I'm so sorry, I never meant to hurt you but I love Evan. I can't marry you. I just can't."

Three of the male wedding attendants approached James and Evan. James told Evan to go on outside.

Will came over to where James was standing. "Why are you here, son?" he asked him.

"He's my best friend, Dad."

"You can't fight these guys in the church, son," Will told him.

"There's only three of them, Dad."

"The operative phrase was 'in the church,' James."

James nodded and winked at Jimmy's three friends, then he turned and headed out the door with Evan.

Will went up to the altar, took his daughter's hand, and walked her back down the aisle. "Sorry, folks, just give us a little time and we'll get this all sorted out."

As Evan and James unceremoniously left the church, they noticed the trooper still waiting by James's truck.

"I guess I'd better go face the music," James said.

"I'll go with you, and I'll pay your fine."

They walked across the parking lot and approached the officer. James started talking immediately. "I'm really sorry, Officer. You see this is my best friend Evan who is also my sister's fiancé. He's been working in Indonesia and—" The officer started to speak but Jamie stopped him. "No, hold on, you see, we thought he was dead. He was reported killed by rebels but it turns out he got away. He got into a river and floated down it a thousand miles—not really that far, but a long way—and he escaped, you see. And my sister thought he was dead so she was about to marry this asshole here in our church. I was speeding to get here, before she could complete the vows and marry the asshole, so she could marry Evan instead, the man she really loves. So, that's why I was—"

The officer held up his hand and James stopped talking. "Slow your roll there, pal," the officer said. "You're giving me a headache. Just tell me one thing. Did you stop the sister from marrying the asshole?"

"*Yes*," both James and Evan shouted at the same time.

"Then go and sin no more," the trooper said. And, with that, he turned quickly, walked back to his cruiser, got into it, and drove away.

James and Evan just stared at each other. "Holy shit," James said, incredulously. "Did that really just happen?"

Then they heard a loud scream coming from the direction of the church. They turned and saw Clare, shoeless, and with her wedding dress pulled up above her knees, sprinting toward them like a track star. She ran up to Evan, jumped into his arms, threw her legs around his waist, planted her lips on his, and left them there for a full thirty seconds. When she finally stopped kissing him, she shouted at him.

"You, asshole, Evan Garner, you see what you almost made me do?" Then she kissed him again.

"I'm sorry, baby, I was dead but I survived it. I love you, Clare."

"You're still an asshole, Evan Garner, but I love you too."

At the church, Will, walked over toward Randall Baxter and motioned to him that he wanted a word with him. Randall approached Will.

"I'm really sorry, Randall. I swear, we thought the boy was dead. Clare has loved Evan since they first met. I'm sorry we had to find out so late and for Jimmy to get hurt."

"You don't have to say you're sorry, Will. I must tell you, watching your girl run across the parking lot and jump into that boy's arms was all I needed to know that, everything that happened here today, was exactly what God wanted to happen. Now my wife and son may be pissed off for a while, but they'll get over that. But you and I are okay. Please give them my best."

"I will, Randall," Will said, "Thank you. I'll take care of any expenses you incurred because of this. That's only fair.

"Not necessary, Will. You paid for the wedding. Jimmy bought his own suit. No amount of money can buy happiness."

"That's true, Randall, thanks again for understanding. Now I must go gather up my chickens and take 'em home." He started walking slowly toward his family waiting in the parking lot.

# About the Author

Jack Sprouse is from Dallas, Texas, although he now lives in Lewisville, a few miles north of Dallas. He studied American History at Texas Tech, in Lubbock, and his fields of greatest historical interest are the American Civil War and World War II. He served in the United States Navy as a crewmember on an ASW (anti-submarine-warfare) patrol aircraft. Writing fiction is his passion.

Sprouse just loves making stuff up (his mom used to punish him for doing that when he was a kid). He has written two books of historical fiction (*Adventures in Time Book I: The American Civil War* and *Adventures in Time Book II: The American West*—these are both Walter Mitty type stories in which he places himself back in time as a war correspondent following historical events and interviewing the major players in those events; two books of original poetry, *The Quiet Place* and *Dreams of a Forgotten Man*—both books contain approximately fifty original poems on various subjects: life, love, friendship, relationships, war, conflict, tragedy; and several novels: *The House Wren*, a saga of a fictional Texas family; *On Nep-*

*tune Wings*, a love story set in the 1960s against the backdrop of a US Navy Patrol Squadron; *Magnolia Road,* an improbable love story between a girl from Vermont and a rancher from Colorado. She is purposeful and dedicated to her chosen calling in life; and *Clare*, about a twenty-four-year-old woman who faces life with quiet confidence and inner turmoil—experiencing love, hurt, uncertainty, sexual harassment in the workplace, and tragedy. He is currently working on several ideas for new books.